Praise for
Michal Ben-Naftali

"This is not a classical Holocaust novel, but rather one
that tries to shed light on the marginal corners of the
period. An important and interesting novel that dares to
take on subjects that are liable to be forgotten."
—Hadar Azran, *Arutz 7*

"A portrait of a woman who defines herself more by 'what she is
not' than by 'what she is,' *The Teacher* tells of guilt, disbelief in
the face of the unthinkable, and the impossibility of a return to
normalcy when everything is crumbling from one day to the next."
—Laëtitia Favro, *Le Journal du Dimanche*

"With a sure hand [Ben-Naftali] transforms her sad
story into an exciting adventure, similar to the discovery
of a new continent. Ben-Naftali handles her heroine,
a survivor devoid of heroism, with reverence."
—The Sapir Prize Committee

"Writing, from Ben-Naftali's point of view, is a
gradual act of redeeming the other."
—Hanna Herzig, *Haaretz*

"This is a lovely, moving novel. . . . There comes a moment,
anticipated but sudden, at which the plot—or the writer's
insights into it—seizes the reader by the throat and
brings them closer to themselves and to the other."
—Yael Geller, *Yedioth Ahronoth*

THE
TEACHER

MICHAL
BEN-NAFTALI

Translated from the Hebrew
by Daniella Zamir

OPEN LETTER
LITERARY TRANSLATIONS FROM THE UNIVERSITY OF ROCHESTER

Library of Congress Cataloging-in-Publication Data: Available.
ISBN-13: 978-1-948830-07-2 / ISBN-10:1-948830-07-8

This book has won the Sapir Prize for Literature and the translation was made possible with the support of The Israel National Lottery

This project and its translation are both supported in part by awards from the National Endowment for the Arts

This project is supported in part by the New York State Council on the Arts with the support of Governor Andrew M. Cuomo and the New York State Legislature

Printed on acid-free paper in the United States of America.

Text set in Garamond, a group of old-style serif typefaces named after the punch-cutter Claude Garamont.

Cover design by Eric C. Wilder
Interior design by Anthony Blake

Open Letter is the University of Rochester's nonprofit, literary translation press:
Dewey Hall 1-219, Box 278968, Rochester, NY 14627

www.openletterbooks.org

THE
TEACHER

"For every image of the past that is not recognized by the present as one of its own concerns threatens to disappear irretrievably."

—Walter Benjamin

1

The sidewalk was cleansed of the blood. Rivers of rain, water hoses, and street sweepers joined forces to scrub the surface after the last remnant was removed. Submissive, the street continued to absorb convoys of people, scraps of paper and cigarette butts hurled absentmindedly in its direction, strollers and bicycles crowding its narrow path. Children played, stumbled and fell, animals evacuated their bowels, garbage cans were tossed back after being emptied. Every so often ambulances rushed by. The fallen leaves piled up and were swept away. Who could remember that stormy night, thirty years ago, when a woman jumped to her death from her rooftop apartment in one of the few still-intact buildings? Of sound mind, with the same parsimonious strictness she used to do everything—pay bills, swim in the pool, or teach, with the same icy ruthlessness she used to drag her long fingernails across the blackboard to force her students to stop making noise—the teacher took her life.

2

No one knew the story of Elsa Weiss. Few called her by name. Most addressed her as one would a general or a sheriff, an authority figure, or a role that she herself created out of thin air and performed with a devotion owed to no one, neither to her superiors nor to those under her supervision, but to something greater and obscure, which she herself perhaps did not fully understand. She was called as one summons the goddess of wrath, a Gorgonteacher, a Fury, subjecting her students to a torrent of tasks, to see if they could take it, if they had the stamina, if she could count on them to hang on, as if she wanted to destroy them to ultimately gain their trust.

Elsa Weiss left no testimony behind. She refused to talk about herself, in fact, refused to discuss anything, to lecture or preach in the classroom. The sphere in which she operated did not expand to infringe on our preferences, influence our fate, shape our moral compass or consciousness. She never relayed to us a cohesive philosophical or political theory that could reveal something of her deep beliefs about knowledge, truth, or faith. Perhaps we could have made assumptions. We could have assumed she was not a woman of faith, that she didn't keep kosher or observe the Shabbat. Her anger wasn't that of a religious person. Or perhaps the opposite was true, despite every fiber of her being shouting defiance. If there was anything religious about her, it manifested in the zeal and extreme fervor with which she performed her tasks, in the ardent belief that accompanied her actions. We could have said that she gave her heart and soul, but what she really gave was something else.

A single photograph, capturing her portrait more or less in her fifties—a rare passport photo taken about two decades after her arrival in Israel—traveled through all the yearbooks, as if it too carried the same consuming quality that seeks to make room for something else, something that isn't a message or a vision, something that lends this word, *teacher*, its very meaning. Her face was a mirror of her life. It bore the pride and severity of someone who rarely talks to another soul, the crushing, tormented face of a Madonna and priestess, once seething with existential angst but now dulled into a blank mask that made you avert your gaze. It was impossible to linger on her face without feeling unsettled.

3

Elsa Weiss made her way to school each morning with swift, efficient strides, without pausing. She probably walked down Dizengoff Street, turning onto Ibn Gabirol up to Sprinzak. Or perhaps she chose the narrower streets, Huberman or Marmorek. And yet, no one actually saw her. No one chanced upon her outside of school hours—in the cafes, the theater, Meir Park, the Beit Ariela public library, where she sat and read for hours on end, in the pool where she swam—no one saw her coming or going. She entered the classroom as if materializing out of thin air, seeking to be left alone, to be seen when she wanted to be seen, invisible when she didn't. And in any event, no one could keep up with her brisk and confident pace, which discouraged accompaniment.

She was about sixty when she was our teacher. Her small, wrinkled face, which could be cupped in one hand, seemed to have been shaped by a sudden blow of old age. The locks of her hair were coiled neatly and meticulously, as if on a potter's wheel, and stacked high into a regal pyramid, elongating her already solemn expression. Had it been released from the dark pin that clasped it, her hair would have reached her waist and created the false impression that it had never been cut or shaved. The bun, towering above a very thin and narrow, flat-looking frame clad in cotton blouses and wool calf-length skirts, lent her a lofty height. Her eyes were a faded green-gray, their color diluted by filmy liquid, but the blue eye shadow she applied enlarged them, brightening her pupils like burning coal. Her fleshy, almost swollen lips—as if bitten too many times—were painted umber, not to say *I am pretty*, or even *I am present*, but to express strength and indignation. The heavy makeup, provoking the very idea of beauty and in complete contrast to the distinguished gray of her clothes, did not seek by way of deliberate embellishment to powder her face into a young and prettier image. It made a different statement: *stay away*, or better yet: *keep your distance*. As if attempting to conceal herself within an alienated body, which greedily gauged her age. However, she did not disguise herself as a teacher. Her disguise was herself, *sui generis*, a battle-seasoned tigress, pretty and ugly, nimble as a doe, despite the fact that no noble animal rhymed with her name, despite the fact that nothing noble was ever associated with her. Her colors were war paint, as if heralding a latent battle in which she was trapped, letting us know that in the center of the microcosm we high school students had founded stood a savage society still foreign to us, a society she embodied with her essence and life experience, without claiming her throne. Had we been children, perhaps we could have appealed to her with rudimentary requests that would have turned her world upside down. But we were teenagers, we revealed nothing more about ourselves than what reluctantly seeped out by dint of our forced coexistence in the classroom.

And yet, she did not allow us to be adolescents. She positioned herself in the midst of youth and at the same time denied it, silencing its voices as if driving them out of the classroom. She did not want to hear anything irrelevant to the curriculum. Our lives were of no interest to her, our origins, our histories, our concerns. She extracted from us an obedient, passive, silent, and unspontaneous quality, as if uprooting us from the realm of youth before we were ready, leaving us floating in an undefined space. We were reticent around her, wore serious demeanors. She would not have us teach her anything, just as she spared us her own story. The wisdom of generations was sealed off from the unknowing wisdom of children, or from the sometimes contrary and uncreative lessons of youth. Life was already behind her, and she was ready to stop in her tracks without taking another step. We were waiting for what still lay ahead of us.

4

We vaguely knew that Weiss had only students, or mainly students. We were her entire world, or most of it, sewn and unraveled anew each year, without everlasting covenants. We knew, but paid it little thought. We were her lifesavers, simply put. Not specifically us, the sophomores, juniors, and seniors of the late seventies—she never adjusted herself to the shifting names and faces—but the essence of it, that same elaborate, well-oiled machine, the classroom, the roll call and protocols, the fixed, reserved manner. She would have none of those surprises that turn a classroom filled with boys and girls into a zoo, an outdoor market or a party. She made sure nothing changed as she dictated the rules, rules which we could actually enjoy when complying with them in full—whether willingly or unwillingly. We never admitted to ourselves that we enjoyed her classes the most, though not in a cheerful or lighthearted way. They went by in a flash, or to be precise: they were at once very slow and very fast. The detached proximity to the students gave her pleasure too, even though she did not allow it to affect her conduct. The joy flitted inside her like an old acquaintance rushing by and waving at her from the other side of the street.

During her classes you could not idle, stare, slip into a lull, or daydream. She expected alertness. We entered the classroom several minutes before class started. We took our seats and prepared for her arrival. We took out our notebooks. On guard, we waited for her to burst in like a tornado, cleaving the room with her steps, perfecting her method that included a mix of cynicism, sarcasm, irony, a raised brow, and a roaring silence with surprising displays of compassion and gentleness. Her pursuit of perfection was cashed into small, tradable coins: proficiency, experience, professionalism, and, outside of class, physical exercise as well. From the few impressions she shared with us about the television programs she watched, it was fairly clear that what sparked her imagination was human nature once it evolved into pure nature, endowed with an innocence that could only be marred by the soul or the spirit.

Most of us didn't breach the distance. It was placed between us and her like the holy of holies. Few risked their lives by crossing over to her bank, with hubris or humility, and even extending their hand to her. Even fewer succeeded. The rest made do with the dense, pulsing contact during class, which preceded an unavoidable short-circuiting later repaired in the following lesson, and again and again. Along the corridors and in the yard we shook our heads with embarrassment. Even if she could be fully trusted, she was unapproachable, impervious to the camaraderie of participation, solidarity, or empathy. She could not be trusted with our secrets not because she wasn't a perfect confidant, but because it was evident she had other things on her mind. We could not pressure her, ask for more, expect more. We never belonged to her, we did not compensate for her lack, we did not arouse her proprietorial instincts. We were never a family to her. There was no room for error on this matter. Her loneliness did not cry out for us. Weiss was a teacher, not a mother. The common reversal in the coming-of-age years, the desire for the teacher to become the mother and take her place, the fantasy that keeps count of the teacher's glances, her hand gliding across your hair, the conversations held with and without words, the desire to conjoin mother and knowledge and, by doing so, break the everlasting covenant between father and knowledge did not apply in her case. None of us were confused about her. She did not force us to feel she was vital to us. In our eyes, the teachers—for there were others as well—embodied that otherness, which stood tall against the obvious conformism in which we grew up. While we might have thought of one as a mutation, three or four women were already a welcome challenge, a way of life, a real possibility. In a generation in which a thick line still divided genders and roles, we learned that you could live a full life without a family, in the traditional sense of the word. You could be around teenagers without being a mother. You could be maternal without being a mother. You could also not be maternal. You could be worlds away from all that, to pass on dry ground as someone else, something else, something we perhaps did not wish to resemble—it was too dark and dangerous, though not necessarily slavish or exilic—but we suddenly knew that it was possible and that it had a different force. These possibilities were cast before us as blunt facts of existence, whether embodied by those who came from there, or those who were born here. Even if the school sought to be a direct extension of the families who sent their sons and daughters there, it also turned its gaze toward a different horizon. We were outside the house. We went to a school that was, by virtue of its team of teachers, extraterritorial.

5

We were "you" to Weiss, second person plural, interchangeable and almost faceless, without distinctions other than the ones created naturally between the stronger and weaker students. She preferred the former, openly favoring them. The praise, however, was modest. She conducted her orchestra without allowing for solos, periodically introducing a first violin or viola, but only when she had had enough, after she had endured an overdose of nonsense that grated on her already overwrought nerves. Then she would call on one of the privileged few to extract an answer. We spoke only when called upon, when the questions asked had answers, ultimate and unyielding. Her questions held no mysteries. She never asked any that were unanswerable, although these saturated dialogues gave us no comfort. We did not exchange opinions with her. The margin of risk was small when she taught, conveying only what was clear and unclassified. Hushed and hesitant, our voices sought approval in the presence of hers, which emerged in a tenor from her droopy lips. That downward tug, contrasting with the heels and the hairdo that pulled upward, was our only glimpse of the insult that life had paid her sometime in her past. At times a scream escaped her mouth. It meant that things were not up for discussion. "You did not do this yourself," she would yell, hurling a thick notebook back at its desk with resolute rage and shooting the student a bone-chilling look. "But, Miss, why don't you believe me? I wrote it myself. I swear," the student would reply, collapsing in her seat and bowing her head, tears of despair already welling up in her eyes. "But, Miss," another student would repeat. "You stay out of this," the teacher would hiss at her, raising her arm as if about to cleave the air in two.

Humiliation was a ceremony. The defendant would rise to her feet, denounced for her failure, and suffer a verbal lashing. We kept silent. There was no point in protesting and undermining Weiss's position, it would only further enrage her and make the display all the more grotesque. We had to let it run its course. She did not enjoy it. She was not a sadist. But she also suffered no qualms or remorse. She never apologized, even when she was wrong. She was beyond reproach. Theories of ethics were the useless vanity of a world that betrayed fundamental principles, a world that could no longer be redeemed. Inside it she was free to stir up violence of mythical proportions, to stage horrors that probably created the only space in which it was possible to live and think. We were terrified of her. We feared her gaze, her vengeance, we feared her petrifying justice, a superior justice that transgressed all the rules she imposed on us, the justice of a guilty survivor tasked with educating guilty generations. Obviously, we were not guilty of murder. We were inherently guilty, guilty of being born, guilty that our lives were normal or could be normal, guilty of our complacent ignorance, which didn't acknowledge that everything could still be turned upside down.

The size of her scream was blatantly disproportionate to the deed. Even she might have agreed with this assessment, had we lived in a world in which we could present her with this question at leisure, after the fact. But in the present her reaction was imbued with the deadly essence of unbiased truth, the senseless howl of an animal, not always escaping voluntarily, although she made sure to lend this eruption the appearance of control, letting it out seemingly by design, releasing it from its cage in full swing only to lock the door again, as if taking pleasure in making us shudder or hurting us, or perhaps in signaling to us that she was beyond pain, beyond shudders. Was all this even directed at us? Did she sense that something was tormenting her and she was, in fact, at its mercy, and right then and there she turned the tables and placed us at her mercy, not because she intended to hurt us, but because she could no longer endure being subjected to someone or something else? Since we knew nothing of the daily battle over her sanity, we viewed it as a kind of demonic outburst. All of a sudden she turned into a volcano of rage. She was not ashamed of it. It did not last long. It ebbed and flowed. We could never predict its appearance, but we knew it would eventually subside. There was always a good reason to be angry. The anger could flare up over a mistake or act of negligence, bad timing, or simply stupidity. Her reaction to these only appeared to be arbitrary. Deep inside her operated a strict logic, from which she could not afford to deviate. The unruly demon emerged when something grated on her nerves, and she, in turn, frayed ours. The shock of her temper made us forget the scene that had triggered the event. The neural moment interrupted our studies like a fire alarm. It was an abrupt test during which we momentarily lost our balance. She, for her part, looked at us with something between triumph and defeat. Was she not aware that she was being violent toward us? Would she, who was so averse to violence, have called her actions violent? Did she really feel threatened? Not because she feared for her skin or her body or her safety, but then, what exactly? Was she trying to shock? To tell us in her own way that violence was out there, lurking wherever we turned, lest we be surprised or naïve? She probably thought she wasn't abusing her power, that she was applying merely moderate pressure in order to yield certain results, and immediately loosened her grip once she obtained them. She employed her authority while loathing authority. She could not help but apply force, without seeking recognition of her power. Despite the combative impression her appearance made, it seemed as though the battles took place all around her, while she herself remained standing in situ, exhausted.

We couldn't imagine how haunted our persecutor was. We knew the drama wasn't limited to the confines of the classroom. We assumed she was being controlled by higher powers. We respected those powers simply because we knew they did not express the growl of arbitrary desires or a futile need for power, because we knew she herself was not her own master. We therefore submitted ourselves to her own submission. We neither enticed nor embarrassed her, neither provoked nor played tricks on her; we did not seek to test her endurance. We did not try to rebel against her, to say no, to refuse to cooperate. We were young, good children, we could withstand her attacks. We did not interpret her actions, we did not make an effort to understand her. She did not have to excuse her behavior to us and we were not entitled to her explanations. We lived in the acute tension she created between reward and punishment, in a space shaped by the threat embodied by her sheer existence.

6

Like any other teacher, Weiss destined herself for the ungratefulness of her students, who were meant, perhaps even expected,
to eventually do better, to exceed her, to forget her in some way.
Her fate supposedly positioned her among those left behind so
we could move forward, those left, in a sense, on the doorstep of
real life, not to cross it but to train others to do so, people who
did not demand our gratitude, unique but replaceable, accepting
as if by divine decree that our world would become richer and
more complex than theirs, that it would exclude them. Like any
other teacher, she lived in horrible fear that everything she had
learned and known, everything she believed in, would be revealed
as useless against the skeptical, dismissive arrogance of her students, for whom thought was still a bold experiment free of form
and considerations. Like in the movie *A Miracle in the Town*, the
first film I saw as a child, over and over, mesmerized, in which the
boys tie their sleeping rabbi to a tree, and he wakes up terrified by
their ropes and his absent authority, not knowing which is stronger, their alertness or his slumber, she too had probably come to
accept the fragility of the relationship, knowing that a circus-like

reversal was in the cards. Fighting in vain to silence our voices, a different teacher, younger and homegrown, picked up her desk and let it drop, the loud thud lingering in the classroom. A desperate rage towered above us when she roared: "There is a limit to a teacher's humiliation," the *R*s rolling out as if in a foreign language. But what suddenly confronted us with the awful possibility of this humiliation—of the humiliated teacher, the teacher who is derided or derides herself once realizing that she is condemned to unbearable disregard, beyond what she had imagined or could afford—what momentarily humbled us, was something that deviated from the logic of daylight to which the school was subjected, six days a week. The incident of the younger teacher's humiliation made us realize the glaring distinction between the subject matter—everyday lessons and morals taught by her and her fellow teachers and quickly forgotten—and the portrait's impression left on us at random, imprinted through her body language and gaze with an intimacy that deviated from the established rules of decency, dormant for years, as if patiently lurking in a dark chamber. An impression that could have remained hidden had it not been revealed inadvertently, through an incident that happened to me, by which I learned that everything, so it seems, is in the service of something else, as if there is still a heavenly design, even though there is neither justice nor judge. An impression that implored me to develop it, to contemplate this portrait and question—have I ever really seen this face, did I see it then as I see it now, with its light washing over me?

7

The years went by and I too became a teacher. I taught literature at one of the high schools in Tel Aviv and, like all teachers, subsisted on a meager salary. I told the students to call me by my first name, as I had introduced myself, and cringed when they chose to address me in a formal manner, as if they were granting me something that wasn't mine. I examined at length the lives forming before me, and partook in them, voluntarily and involuntarily. The age gap between us widened. I sought to stop the passing of time, I erected floodgates against change. From that insufferable thing I accumulated, often called experience, I could witness the agonies of adolescence down to the finest facial expression. I did not always dare ask myself how they viewed me. I feared they attributed to me advantages life had actually deprived me of, I was frightened of the power I held, I wanted them to size me up accurately. I was familiar with the Eros sustaining the relationship, I made sure to learn their names by heart. I tried opening the windows, not to seal, not to blind, not to coerce. I would arrive in the classroom early. On rare occasions I immediately sat at my desk near the blackboard. I knew that once I sunk heavily into the chair, it was a foreboding sign, a sign of fatigue, a sign that I would not be able to speak a word that day, that I would sit bare and depleted, the words would emerge like ghost emissaries of another spirit. Through an unspoken pact, it seemed they understood that something was being told to them in a secret language. Because that's what I learned with time, that there is a secret language between teachers and students, neither sufficiently deciphered nor consciously registered. I leafed through my papers absentmindedly, my gaze resting upon crammed paragraphs I had jotted down without being able to disentangle them during class. I didn't know how to hide. Daydreams fought for my attention and conquered substantial areas of my consciousness while I adamantly sought to talk about other things. I often switched off and couldn't be a teacher, unless I was a teacher then too, more of a teacher than at any other time. I was a teacher when I could be and I was a teacher when I couldn't be, a teacher when I could help it and when I was helpless. I taught helplessness, I sat with it in their company. I removed my glasses and saw blurry figures. I tossed words into the air, speaking to no one in particular, wondering what I was conveying to them; I assumed that students, their gaze accompanying the teacher's hand gestures and body language, recognized something profound in the empty source of her words, without being familiar with her private life; that their ears were tuned into the inflection, the melody, into what she was saying and what she was not saying. Every so often, at the end of class, I was presented with a student's sketch of me, which interestingly enough was never realistic. Usually it was an expressionist sketch that flooded what was bubbling beneath the surface, that same past I had given them despite my intentions, a past that is not the historical past, which they could probably read about in books, but the one I saw, the one I experienced, what I understood about myself and about others. All those years I knew that I myself was still searching for a teacher, that I had not yet called off the search. I searched for a teacher desperately. I searched for the teacher. I wanted to know what the lesson was that only few could teach, or that only one in particular could teach.

I don't know whether what I am about to relay is indeed about her. I imagine it probably is, but I can't be one hundred percent certain and I am not sure I wish to explore further. I am not sure I really want to know. I am not built for research; I admit that I have no investigative instincts, or what they call "intuition." My knowledge is of a different kind, the knowledge of what might have happened, or rather, what should have happened and most likely did happen to the one who went to the point of no return. I had no need to talk about it with anyone, not out of vanity; I wanted to tread beside the facts, not lean on them. I sought to touch the margins of what had happened, something I imagined was close to reality, yet fell short of it. On one occasion (and I will soon elaborate), she stood by me and almost without turning her head said: *Look at me. Just once. Without questions. Try to describe what you see. Use your freedom.* But how does one use freedom? No one had told me her story. A few people knew some of it, tiny fragments that never formed a sequence. But I know. I know that she was born on 1917, that she passed away in 1982, that she parted from her parents in July of 1944. I know that she crossed oceans and continents. I know everything and nothing at all. Oh well, I tell myself. From this point forward, it is all fiction.

8

She used to wake up at four-thirty in the morning without an alarm clock, drink a cold glass of water in one long sip, and put on her one-piece bathing suit with flowers printed in red, blue, and white, like the French flag—a choice not without whimsy— with a U-back design that let the breeze brush against her skin; during those long days of summer break in which she abandoned the pool for the beach, she would lie exposed to the sun that still showed mercy toward her withered, lean body, indulge in the soft grains of sand that sent a sweet shiver through her bones, and then go into the water and tease the waves, closing her eyes, turning her back on them, bending her neck, submitting to their authority and letting them carry her to safe shores. During the school year she would take the canvas bag that awaited her at the entrance to her apartment, shove a clean towel, swimming cap, and her purse inside it and scurry down the three flights of stairs, rushing north to the end of her street and turning left toward the sea, to Gordon Pool. Summers and winters, Shabbats and holidays, Elsa Weiss was summoned by the pure saltwater like a devout Jew to the morning Shacharit prayers. She greeted the guard at the entrance, gave a reserved smile to the few bathers who managed to arrive before her, placed her bag in her locker and sat at the end of the pool for a brief moment of meditation before diving in. Empty of all thoughts, Elsa Weiss swam twenty laps, her firm legs and muscular arms cutting through the water with fixed and elaborate strokes, propelling her forward inside the thawing element, her lips pursed like those of a fish, contained in her silence. Later she would quickly pat herself dry with the stiff towel, put on her light cotton dress and dash back to her apartment. She would stop by the grocer's near her building. He would already have her salami sandwich and pickle waiting. She added milk and sweetener to the tab—"What do you need sweetener for, Ms. Weiss, with a body like yours?" the grocer would tease her—yogurt, sliced cheese and a few vegetables for a salad she would prepare when she returned from school. "The usual?" "The usual. Put it on my account. I'll pay you at the end of the month." "No problem, Ms. Weiss. Have a good day." And already she's climbing the stairs to her apartment, spreading out the *Haaretz* newspaper she had removed from the mailbox, opening the window facing the backyard to let the air in, putting on the kettle, pouring herself a cup of black coffee and spreading a thin layer of butter and blueberry jam on two pieces of toast. The radio is broadcasting the seven o'clock news; student papers are piled at the end of the dining room table; she reminds herself to shake off the crumbs before putting them in a folder; sometimes she forgets. The small traces of bread and occasional grease stains suggest, to our relief, that she is taking care of herself.

9

She did not wake up with firm resolutions. They lunged at her on her way to school and she served as their holy instrument. She offended and crushed and seemingly enjoyed the awe she inspired behind her back, or perhaps was unable to gauge the vulnerability of those whose daily bread was not pain and suffering. No, she would not give anyone the pleasure of loving her, she did not care one bit if she was loved or not, all the better, she would be the disliked teacher; she would be intolerable and set their teeth on edge, jar their ears and upset their balance until they climbed the walls.

We learned because we were afraid, not because we loved her; we submitted more than we complied, but it is possible that we did not recognize that learning was a gift we presented in her honor. In the courtyard by the school we fought about her with passion and anger, but even behind her back we preserved her honor. We did not call her cruel names. To those who remained silent during these arguments, or at least weren't quick to respond, Weiss was in some odd way too intimate a subject. They could not begin to explain it, not even to themselves. It's possible that they were struggling for their present, or even their future. The future was the teacher, and more specifically, the future was that quality she possessed, a quality that placed the exceptional in our midst, not as a miracle or wonder, but as a gleaming possibility. The exceptional was possible. Since she did not deliver sermons, she left, in a sense, only herself, who she was, the gradually fading memory of her. She was an axis on the world map, the South or North Pole, alternatingly too hot and too cold, a pole that awaited us at the end of a journey that could have been fated or meaningless. There were no tears there, in these parts. It was dry as a desert. We couldn't know anything about it. She, on the other hand, could neither describe it nor invite us in, and perhaps she did not wish us to ever come near this territory. It was hers, her lot in life. She did not want to teach from within it, to turn it into a profession, but neither could she be a teacher from outside it.

10

Elsa Weiss taught English. The grease that occasionally smeared the tests and papers she corrected alluded to the ethics of manual labor, the ardor of a craftsman or peasant who never missed a day's work. The English slowed down the communication. It also veered her off her straight path. If any words of truth were spoken in it, they were simple, basic words that circumvented anything that was important to say. The English language disguised her insult and replaced it with a mode of communication whose discursive units allowed for shared practice, correction, and improvement. A hidden treasure, a language always has something to teach; we might abuse it, manipulate it to lie, distort, dirty our mouths, deceive others as well as ourselves, but at least with Weiss we'd learn how to use it properly. English enabled her to create a coherent space. One word stood in for another word, a synonym. But her world deviated from any translation. Nothing could be inferred about her internal grammar from the dictionary we memorized. She did not teach what she had learned firsthand, as if the teacher had to shed herself from herself in order to teach, as if learning and teaching had to come from different facets of her being, in a foreign language, a language she undoubtedly commanded, but not a full command, and one she never treated as her own. As if she had imposed on herself to forever be foreign, an outsider in the place that had become her home, in the medium and in the subjects she taught. She thought you could be a teacher without betraying a thing, with a kind of blanched hypocrisy meant to protect her and her students. She had placed a heavy burden on herself, but it was not a matter of restraint. It was a strict forbiddance she deliberately imposed on herself, as if understanding she must not draw her students close to the voids that her teachings concealed. There were certain things they didn't need to know, lest they imagine it was within their power to save her. And the teacher knew no one could really save her.

She became the one to whom that thing had happened, and we, born a generation after her, in a different country, on a different continent, what could we possibly have understood? We could be lured in. Others lured us, she despised it. She also found no use in pointing out numbers or drawing battle maps. Putting it in our mouths meant risking it might be corrupted, not because we were corrupt, but because we simply had no clue. She developed tactics to sidestep, to cover up, to conceal. Nothing slipped out of her mouth for no reason, inadvertently or by mistake. Once, unexpectedly, following an article we had read together in the *Jerusalem Post*, she lingered on the word Nazism. "What is 'Nazism'?" her voice carried across the classroom. Silence prevailed. She looked at us with either despair or disdain, and for a moment it seemed she was considering what to say. "Well?" "National-Socialism," I finally dared to reply with a feeble voice. It is likely that everyone knew what Nazism was. It wasn't a matter of knowledge. Something else had prevented the others from speaking. In order to answer, we had to momentarily ignore the fact that it pertained to her. The silence of the others was no less essential than my "correct answer." Both were attentive to the tremor in Weiss's voice.

11

Nevertheless, she qualified to teach French.

"Do you know that in Paris they drink coffee from bowls, not mugs, and they dunk the croissant in it?" she said, accompanying her words with modest, somewhat sensual hand gestures. That was all she ever said about pre-war Paris, where she arrived by train from Budapest in order to study French. From her year-long stay at the Ladagnous boarding house on rue d'Assas, abutting Luxembourg Gardens, from everything she saw and learned there, from all the people she met, she cherished this insignificant image, a piece of the past that did not connect to a thing, and yet she felt it could be shared and experienced, this ritual dipping of bread, this freedom to taste. Paris was encapsulated in this moment that stood out in its triviality, its leisure, because it conveyed nothing but itself, because it did not betray the period in which—apart from the momentary aggravation inflicted by the mustached, surly housemother who opened the boarding house gate to her with quiet imprecations, scolded her, "You're late," and waved her and her heavy suitcase up the five steep flights of stairs—she was truly happy. She was twenty years old, the same age her mother had been in the photo she placed on the desk, a photo taken on a rare occasion during which her mother was not hiding behind her thick glasses, her dark eyes piercing the camera lens. Beside her she placed a photo of her father and Jan, taken a few weeks before Jan left for Palestine. She preferred to keep Eric's photo in her purse. Since she was so efficient and calculated with her words, they sounded more like an interval that signaled an area that was off limits, a space where only in hindsight could you notice its utopian "before" quality, a moment equivalent to dipping something sweet in hot liquid, an otherworldly life, a life that told us that she, the teacher, lived a Madeleine cookie, whose virtue does not necessarily belong to early childhood but to the egress from childhood, a virtue that carries a promise, that offers an outlet of foreignness.

12

"*Ver hot aza meydele / A malekhl a sheyns? Oygn vi tsvey shterndlekh / A neshomele a reyns.*" Father hums Herman Yablokoff's song, which he heard from a colleague at school, while shuffling the cards with dazzling speed. He fans out four jacks, a heart and a club, a diamond and a spade, and places the king on top—their father. "Once upon a time there were four princes," he begins. "They grew up with their father the king alone in the palace. One day the king was summoned to war. He convened his sons in the parlor and announced: 'My sons! My sons! I was called to the battlefield. I do not know when I shall return. I trust you to safeguard the wings of our palace from all harm.'" She stands on tiptoe, watching him suspiciously: "One son," he says while waving the jack of hearts before her eyes, "will guard the wine cellar. This way," and he flips the card and quickly inserts it into the deck slightly above the bottom. "The second son will guard the treasure chamber." He takes the jack of clubs, flips and sticks it in a bit higher up the deck. "The third son will guard the fort." Now the jack of diamonds disappears into the realm of the task assigned to him. "And the fourth son will guard the

34

king's stables." The deck swallows the youngest son too, the jack of spades. "Many moons go by," Father continues, "until the king returns home with a victor's glory. Upon his return he exclaims: 'My sons! My sons!'" Now she must follow his movements closely. "And the four princes came sliding down the chimney." Father confidently dangles jack after jack from the top of the deck. Her eyes nearly pop out of her head. "But Father," she says, "how do you do it?!" She picks up the deck and considers it at length. She flips through the cards with her strong fingers in an attempt to find more hidden layers. "Not with force," he says, smiling. "Force will not help you here." "Like this?" she asks, and gently stirs the cards. He nods. She looks at him skeptically and shrugs. The magic is over. He promises that in a year he will teach her several ancient Georgian spells he learned from Rabbi Deutsch. "Why not now?" she protests. Years later she remembered how he fulfilled his promise and taught her, that following year, how to perform the trick she liked the most, the mind reader, Nauka-Mnogo-Umeet-Gitik, which she learned by heart—Father had told her to destroy all written evidence—and how, when she tried the trick on Eric one day, he immediately sat down to work out the arithmetic behind it. But who even wants to decipher magic, she thought.

They invited the Adlers over for afternoon tea, to celebrate her sixth birthday with the family. Clara, their young daughter, goes to school with her. Elsa is almost twice her width and height. Clara's parents do not allow them to horse around outside because they say, so Clara has told her, that Elsa is "a menace, a troublemaker, a little hooligan." Mrs. Adler, who heard from Mrs. Bloom, Elsa's mother, that Elsa had been expelled from kindergarten after untying the shoelaces of all the children, said she "wasn't the least bit surprised." Elsa was just passing through the living room. Mrs. Adler looked at her and repeated: "I'm not the least bit surprised." It wasn't exactly the birthday she had been hoping for. Clara announces to her on the doorstep: "My mother told me to bring your gift to school tomorrow. She said I don't need to bring two gifts." Elsa doesn't understand why, if you're invited to two separate celebrations, you don't need to bring two gifts, but she'll ask Jan what he thinks later. Jan has "observations" about people, and always has smart things to say about Mr. and Mrs. Adler.

"*Ver hot aza meydele*," she sings cheerfully, dispelling the gloom that had befallen her, and pulls Clara toward the kitchen to eat candy. "You want me to make you chocolate milk?" she offers. "You know how to make chocolate milk?" Clara asks, looking at her with admiration. "Sure, of course, I made it tons of times." It is a test, and she's certain she remembers all the stages. She places two glasses on the counter, puts a teaspoon of cocoa powder and two teaspoons of sugar in each glass, holds them under the faucet for water and adds milk from the jug in the pantry. She stirs vigorously for a long time. The mixture refuses to dissolve and looks lumpy and strange. She hands Clara a glass. "Drink," she says. Clara grimaces. "Yuck, you're disgusting." "Maybe we should try again?" she suggests, and before Clara responds, she repeats all the stages anew. Why can't she get it right? She's already six.

Mr. Adler says they look bored and proposes a riddle. Elsa hates Mr. Adler's riddles, which only his daughter can solve. Jan tells Elsa that her own solutions simply aren't economical, and that they attest to a "deficit in mathematical thinking." Where it is possible to encumber, she encumbers, to prolong, she prolongs, to complicate, she complicates. The whole idea, he tells her, is to find the shortcut. She knows she falls for every trap, and this time, on her birthday, she doesn't feel like falling. Last year her parents invited Ms. Kárpáti, a witch who became renowned in the Jewish community of Kolozsvár for the tales she spun, a real Jewish Scheherazade, acclaimed also for her riddles. To the circle of girls that formed around her, Ms. Kárpáti told a riddle about an eight-year-old boy who, according to her, was a bookworm. Day and night he devoured books until he became pale and weak. His worried parents tried to limit his reading hours so that he would get enough sleep, but the child tried to trick them. Hearing his parents' footsteps outside his room at nine-thirty, half an hour after lights-out, he hid the book underneath his pillow, turned off the lamp beside his bed and feigned sleep. Now, Ms. Kárpáti shrilled, how did the parents know, upon approaching the child's bed, that he was not really sleeping but merely pretending? Indeed, how could they know? Elsa asked herself with wonder. "Oh. Piece of cake," the freckled, yellow-haired Eva replied. "The lamp was hot." "Correct," Ms. Kárpáti confirmed and presented Eva with a prize, a homemade chocolate pomegranate she always carried with her in a basket when performing. The simpler the answer—the more it required straightforward logic and the power of deduction—the further it eluded Elsa, her mind a jumble of loose thoughts. What else could she do but memorize the words? "The lamp was hot." The lamp was probably the main suspect and all her nightly activities ought to be carried out in the darkness. In the dark she seats her favorite teddy bear and tells him about her day. In the dark she whispers her wishes into the pillow. In the dark she dreams dreams. Sometimes, when she's sick, Jan hides candy for her under her mattress, in the dark. Jan also knows he must get her away from the Adlers. He promised to whistle the family whistle from the top of the street to let her know that the youth group meeting was over, and that today he was not going to allow anyone to embarrass her.

In the meantime she finds refuge in Father's song and the magic trick from last night. "*Liber got, ikh bet bay dir*," she hums. The previous evening, when he tucked her in and wished her a happy birthday, her lips brushed against his face and inadvertently touched his lips. He is the handsomest of all fathers. She has absolute confidence in that. "You're always bragging about your family," Clara often teases her. "You never stop talking about them. You go on and on, my father and my brother, my father and my mother." She wonders whether she indeed talks about them more than other children. If, heaven forbid, someone said anything bad about Jan, she could kill them. And then it happens. "What I feared has come to pass," as Father says. "I heard Jan got kicked out of school," Clara says. She feels as if the rug has been pulled out from under her feet. "Kicked out? Where did you hear such nonsense?" "I heard it at home," Clara says and offers no more. Elsa takes a deep breath. "He's a counselor for the Zionist youth group, and the school principal, Doctor Dankner, doesn't like it. He says it's a bad influence on the students." "That's exactly what I heard, a bad influence," Clara enthuses. "Clara, do you even know what you're talking about?" Her eyes are welling up. "He's a straight-A student," she immediately adds. "That has nothing to do with it," Clara replies. The conversation is suffocating her. At home they have heated arguments about it. Father, who runs the Neolog elementary school in Kolozsvár, lost his temper when he first heard. Jan replied harshly that if he is not "backed" at home then maybe he really should rush to follow his "calling." These words are a riddle, but she can toss them at

Clara with ease: "He has backing and a calling," she sums it up. Clara stares at her at length without saying a word. If Elsa really wants to be nasty, she has a trump card, but she's saving it for a time of need; "only when the situation is no longer bearable," Jan had cautioned her. She knows from Jan that Clara's sister is a "complete idiot" and perhaps even repeated a grade. But that's nothing—they say her father is involved in the black market. She heard her parents talking about it at home. What's the black market? It's serious trouble. But Father is his friend. So perhaps it is best to leave it alone. And in any case, one shouldn't be quick to offend people. It's a shame her mood was ruined. If Clara says one more word, she'll fight her. Clara isn't as strong as her, but she has long fingernails that can gouge her skin. Elsa fixes her light eyes on her. She thinks Clara is a very pretty girl. "Truce," she suggests. Clara accepts happily. And then the sound of the whistle cuts through the air. Elsa almost bursts into laughter. She runs out of the apartment, her legs carrying her as if on their own accord, galloping toward her "cavalier," like Grandma Rosa says.

13

Odd how it all suddenly came flooding back, on her way home to Tel Aviv from Bat Yam. More than fifty years had gone by, and she never remembered exactly what had happened. She recalled a certain exertion in her hands, her arms, recalled that she was doing something strange. No, it only turned out to be strange later, at the time it had simply happened. The ill-at-ease feeling awakened in her only decades later, after denying the entire story, after believing that she had forgotten and that she had nothing left, that everything had been destroyed in the great fire that consumed the apartment in Tel Aviv, that the fire had swallowed the books, the photographs, the letters, that she had no image left to hold onto, after she tried to extract images from within and—nothing, ashes upon ashes, only then had she invoked that image from the abyss. It was night time and her parents were out, probably visiting the Adlers. Perhaps they had taken Grandma Rosa with them. Jan was away at summer camp for a few days and let her sleep in his bed. She was frightened, something had woken her from her sleep, maybe she had heard noises outside and had gotten up, drowsy, to see what was going on, if the door was indeed locked, and on her way back to bed mistook the bathtub for the toilet. She sat down on the slippery rim, gripping it, but sensing the absence of the backrest and that she might easily slide and collapse into the concave bathtub, she pressed her hands against the opposite wall with all her might, pushed her body up, rushed back to bed, and sank into a deep sleep. She remembered that in those days the boys had let her into their secret club, after she had successfully passed several clandestine tasks she had not told a soul about, not even Jan, who was her confidant, and even got to participate in a meeting on the roof of Janusz's house by the school, in which they embarked on a pursuit of MWTBC, the encrypted name of the man-with-the-black-cape who chased them around town. Short Albert said in his determined baritone that the man was plotting to kill them, and they had to outrun him. The gravity of the mission had scared her, and she leaned back on a pile of bricks that was placed in front of their headquarters to settle her racing heart. "Are you crazy?" Albert roared. "You're leaving fingerprints. We'll all be found out because of you." She quickly shoved her hands deep into her pockets. Albert's instincts and swift reaction troubled her. While she contemplated what to do, Jóska, Albert's right hand man, brought down his fist on her. She swore to the boys she would not rat on them, that they could trust her completely, and when she returned home with her left eye ringed in crimson, she adamantly refused to tell the truth, and said she was playing with a ball and stumbled into the goalpost. Was she afraid she would talk about it and betray them in her sleep? Was it that fear that woke her up? Or perhaps it was the tension that prevailed in the house over Jan's imminent departure and the realization that they would not see each other for a long time, even though they had stopped talking about it, maybe because they understood there was no way to talk about it, because it was impossible to grasp or plan, it deviated from the time units familiar to her, and so it seemed to her parents as well; but the impending trip already cleaved the air, and Father and Jan, like old warhorses, had put down their weapons. Father tried to listen attentively to the plans of the young pioneers, as he called them, regarding Palestine, and outside the house he even spoke with pride about his son's independence and determination, "a stand-up boy," he said about him behind his back. For some reason it was not enough to alleviate her concerns, because the mere conflict was more than she could bear; it was a fact, Jan was leaving, which meant that someone couldn't live with someone, someone had to give up and go away, there were things, she understood, that could not coexist and there could be no compromise between them. Jan explained to her that Mother and Father could not live with his truth, and he, for his part, could not live with theirs. "Parents always identify with authority, because it upholds their authority and because they mistakenly believe that we, the children, need authority, that without it we cannot grow." "You're an authority to me," she said to him. "You're right," he replied with a smile, "but one day, I hope, you will rebel against me." Was she really capable of rebelling? She wondered. She often heard Father tell Mother that he was skeptical about the whole Zionist thing. He would not get up and leave everything they had here for any "spiritual" fortune— not to mention "material" fortune. "What do you have here?" Jan asked derisively. He did not believe that the atmosphere of anti-Semitism and terror that prevailed around them was worthy of the name "home." Elsa had no doubt that for her and her parents it was home. It was difficult to understand how you could leave it, and for such a faraway place. "What if you regret it?" she asked him. "When you grow up, you'll join me," he promised her. "You certainly can't stay here for long."

The following morning she discovered she had relieved herself in the bathtub. Father was hunched over the cramped bathroom sink, letting it fill with water while Mother stood behind him and relayed the awful, terrible story. "The smell when we came back from the Adlers," she said. "And what was it? You can't imagine, like a horse's." And she waved her hand in a snake-like motion as if painting how it looked, a gesture that conveyed both wonderment and disgust. "I swear it wasn't me," Elsa said, defeated, but there was no sign that someone had broken into their apartment. "Admit it, at least admit it was you." "Why? It wasn't me!" Mother sighed heavily and started scrubbing the bathtub again, having already cleaned it the night before, and then proceeded to dust and sweep every room. Father let the "Minister of Interior," as he called her, supervise all household matters. Apart from birthdays, those rare occasions during which she was allowed to invite a group of children, she was permitted to host only one friend at a time, and invite her to stay for dinner, provided they reported to the sink immediately upon finishing their meal, their hands raised in a gesture of salutation or submission, so as not to smear oil on the chairs or soil the walls and thus sabotage the immaculate cleanliness which Mother had accomplished through constant housework that calmed her. She remembered her tantrums over Jan's "vulgar" posters, which he had the nerve to hang in "her house." Jan fought back. He said that his room was his castle and that she had no right to meddle in whatever happened inside it. "You can never achieve perfection," he teased her. "To stop making a mess is to stop living." He groused to Elsa that sometimes it seemed to him that Mother's obsessive cleaning was her statement against life, that she was picking a fight with it to loosen its grip on her. But what kind of battle is that? Elsa asked. Jan said he believed Mother was battling life because she felt she had no foothold on it.

She remembered that around that time, more or less, she refrained from arguing with Mother and did almost all she could to appease her, anything to keep her from yelling. Not because Mother shouted more than other mothers—she could hear Mrs. Adler yelling at her daughters all the way from the town square— but because her shouts had a different quality, and always sounded like an echo chamber for a stifled cry that filled Elsa with dread. It was as if the shouts were a distraction to disguise something else that refused to be exposed, perhaps her frustrating idleness, maybe her mute resentment toward Grandma Rosa, who had become dependent on them day in and day out since her husband passed away, when Elsa was seven. To her question why Mother had given Grandma Rosa a free pass, Father explained that was how a daughter should treat her mother: "That is the meaning of honoring thy parents." But it seemed to her that Mother was acting out of a sense of duty and did not truly love Grandma Rosa, because apparently love could not be commanded. This realization caused her distress, and to fear that Mother was acting out of a duty toward Father, or even to her. And even though she believed it was different in their case, she was not entirely sure. At times Mother's rage was directed at Father or Jan or her, but maybe that was a sign of unconditional love? "There is no such thing as unconditional love," Jan claimed. "Love is always conditional. Whoever says otherwise is indulging in puerile romantic fantasies. If you can't explain to yourself why you love the thing you love, then ultimately you love it because you have decided to, and what you love is actually love itself." She looked at him with gleaming eyes. She actually liked that idea, loving love itself.

She knew that when Jan left, she would remain alone with Father and Mother and Grandma Rosa, and no one would be there to save her. Grandma had no respect for Mother, she listened to her with only half an ear, nodding skeptically, and talking to her with an affected tone as if sizing her up, perhaps even embarrassed by her. But Mother ignored it as if already accustomed to her behavior, and replied with a flat matter-of-factness that only rarely was darkened by discontent. It was unclear whether Mother actually heard what Elsa heard, whereas Grandma was blind to Elsa's gaze, which studied her cautiously and contemplated how to come between them and prove to Grandma that Mother was more important than her. She wondered whether they had ever had a real conversation, and whether such a conversation could even take place, with Grandma always ordering Mother around as if she knew better what was proper and what was improper.

Mother came from an Orthodox family. When they heard the rumors that the Romanian authorities were about to close down the Hebrew high school, thus ending the cooperation between the Orthodox and the Neologs, Grandma Rosa pressured Mother into sending Elsa to the religious school. Father, who also thought Mother did too much to please Grandma Rosa, adamantly objected to the idea. He feared it would "torture the girl and put her in an impossible conflict with our way of life." After all, you yourself pulled away from them, he reminded Mother. Religious education was ill-suited to Elsa's curious and free-spirited character and might depress her, or even radicalize her, because "that is the nature of such processes. You saw what happened when

Glasner Junior inherited Glasner Senior's place! The successful sons always pull toward the extremes, while the others are feeble and incompetent." And his girl is far from feeble. He feared what would happen to the family once they were torn between the Orthodox, Neologs, and Zionists, each with his own *Mikveh* and butcher and Torah. It could not be divided in such a manner. "It will give her structure," Mother insisted. "She must have structure. She can't play all day." "May she continue to play, as long as that's what she wants. She'll have enough time to be serious."

In hindsight, she marked this morning as "the morning after." It more or less resembled every morning that had preceded it. She was already in the third grade. The teachers were fond of her, even though they complained that she was impertinent and opinionated; and when she wasn't busy expressing all manner of opinions—about grades, the Orthodox, God, and whatnot (she heard Mother parroting her to Father: "This is how your daughter speaks," she rebuked, hurling at him sentences that Elsa had recited and putting her to shame by exposing these clumsily and prematurely-adopted adult mannerisms), she could be found doubled over with laughter, causing a chain reaction of giggling children until there was no other choice but to send her outside to calm down. Everything made her laugh, the teacher's barrel-shaped body, her voice that sounded like a croaking toad, the laughter of others, Jan's whistles when he paid her a surprise visit. "As far as I'm concerned, let her laugh her entire life," Father said. Outside the house she was also prone to vexation. At times, she did not know what had come over her. Leah, her Torah teacher, wrote in her second grade yearbook: "Without anger and petulance you are as lovely as a flower." What did she see in her, Miss Leah? What did she grant her with that mysterious sentence, etched in her heart without having to be memorized, even though she was inclined to fight its refined truth, which she only partially unraveled? But you can neither question memories nor seek apologies, not after that instance in which Sonichka, the gangly girl from her grade, wrote her a Rosh Hashanah greeting: "To Elsa, have a good year, with happiness, joy, and a little cheer," and Elsa allowed herself to wonder out loud, "Why did you write only 'a little cheer'?" to which Sonichka replied, "For the rhyme."

She didn't know why she was so gloomy that morning. Perhaps because she had experienced for the first time something she would one day identify as the price of adjustment, a type of interim state that enabled her to function at a steady, confident pace, rattled only when encountering fervor or passion in others, and because she had long sensed in herself that greediness, she could not help but notice the gap suddenly opening up between her and them. It was also the gradual, obscure realization that the words of her bearers were creating her anew, no less than their bodies had created her.

Since she could first remember, Mother forbade her to get dirty or lie. She claimed splitting yourself in two was a sin and that she must strive to be a good girl, an open book. "Wears her heart on her sleeve," Mother said admiringly of one of her friends at the *Ozer Dalim* charity organization, who wasn't a hypocrite like most of the women around her. Elsa had failed the "honesty test," as Mother called the bathtub incident, with a harsh voice and a long, distinct pause between the two words, as they were walking in their Shabbat clothes down the main street with Grandma Rosa to synagogue. Elsa looked dizzily at the rounded steeples of the elegant building, which from afar resembled crystal balls; hesitant drops of urine escaped into her underwear, once she realized that what had happened between them was known to all.

From then on, she let the mission take over her soul. Even when she tried to lie, she was no longer successful. She became transparent and her innermost thoughts could be read. During Torah study, when they studied the Book of Genesis, she thought that evil was actually created with a word, just as God had created the sun and the moon and the stars and the people. Words generated actions, which meant there would be no evil deeds were people like Mother or Leah not to call every mischief by such a cruel name. She could actually prove from Genesis that the word evil always appeared before the evil deed, as if the word spurred one into action. But she felt the adults understood nothing about words, even though their vocabulary was much larger than hers. That was why they squandered words recklessly, and stood astonished when they suddenly turned into reality, while she, for her part, could no longer endure it. "Can't you simply forget what I said? It's just a word." Mother shrugged her off when she got hung up on some offending word. "Let it go, just ignore her," Jan said when she complained to him, endorsing the advice she had received. "She's simply stupid, and you, with your reaction to her, are just punishing yourself." But it seemed to her that he was disrespecting Mother, and that she certainly couldn't bear, not without immediately turning herself into the object of that ridicule. After all, she was her daughter. How could she outsmart herself? Only years later did she realize that was precisely the reason she had conferred a special validity upon Mother's words, thus rendering her important, or perhaps a monster. And Mother was not a monster, she was an ordinary woman, so why had Elsa given her so much power, and why had she resigned herself to relinquish it? Perhaps it was the lurking fear of her own power that led her to form an alliance with the prohibitions imposed on her. Perhaps because deep down she had already broken every possible command, had seen unholy sights, and had come into knowledge too early, she subconsciously decided not to know more.

Many years later, when it seemed she withdrew entirely from the child she had been—when there was nothing left of her other than that furtive vestige that bemused her when she wondered where she had disappeared to—she dreamt she was living in a spacious house, its many rooms unoccupied. Her parents enter her room and tear pictures off the walls, picture after picture, as if behind each picture was another. They are looking for something. She is convinced she has murdered someone or something. Suddenly someone emerges from under the floorboards, points at her and explains that she herself has been murdered, but she insists she is to blame. She has caused someone to no longer exist and from that moment on she has been covering it up, laying fabric, and all that faded long ago and then went up in flames in the big fire. Now she does not remember a thing, not the person in question, not the circumstances of the murder, how it went unsolved, how she has not been exposed. She has forgotten it all. But suddenly she was outed by her own self and could no longer hide.

She remembered the day she helped Jan pack his books, how she climbed on a chair to clear the top shelf and stumbled upon a book by someone named Lukács and sat down to leaf through it, a book Jan must have hidden far from their parents' reach, a philosopher Jan's friends often argued about while she hung out in his room, when she wasn't sent out on urgent tasks, when the girls curled up in the boys' laps like kittens and the voices faded into whispers and giggles, and they realized that Elsa was no longer playing but hanging her head low and staring at the floor, seeking to escape the embarrassment that had overcome her. From what she could gather from their conversation, Lukács had tried to secularize Hungary by advocating free love and protesting against the authority of the prudish Church, against parents and teachers who preached modesty, against "monogamy," a word that appeared in the table of contents which she made a note to herself to ask Jan about, when just then Mother walked into the room and snatched the book from her hands. "You're too young for this," she snapped at her. "Can't you make yourself useful instead of rifling through Jan's books?" Elsa was staring at the page in front of her, and her mother's sentence turned, as if by magic, into a command that precluded any reflection, casting out sex, sexuality, and "radical sexual education" with a silence not to be reckoned with.

About four years after Jan's departure, she met a young Gentile, three years her senior, who swam with her at the municipal pool. They saw each other often and spent many afternoons strolling through the botanical gardens. Georg was planning to study biology at Franz Joseph University upon graduating from high school, and dreamt of writing a book about "life on earth," a book that would have no people in it, but only creatures at various stages of development, from the most primitive to the most complex creature, because the world of living creatures interested him infinitely more than people, and truth be told, he tended to place humanity at the very bottom of the evolutionary chain. His father had fallen in World War I, several months before he was born. He utterly distrusted human beings and knew all too well what they were capable of doing to each other. One evening, while her parents were out visiting friends, Elsa invited him over. They stood on the apartment balcony and gazed onto the street beyond the railing. Georg approached her from behind and gently stroked her hair. With courteous yet tenacious confidence his fingers slowly descended and playfully looped around her earlobes, then lower to massage her neck and brush against her breasts; she conceded to his silent calls, her ears filling with the sound of cymbals that crescendoed as he crowded his body against her behind. "I love it when you tremble," he said. They didn't hear the key turning in the front door lock.

She was to break off the relationship at once. The girls in school knew she had been involved with a Gentile. They spoke of her behind her back. Since that night, during which she dreamt about Georg's body with longing, she could conjure up no images. All she could remember was the immediacy with which pleasure was dangled before her and then taken away, like a now that appeared as a once-upon-a-time. Her mind was devoid of figures and fantasies; sometimes she looked inside herself and saw exposed body parts, to which nothing clung, no story, no movement, no character. She discovered she was easily aroused, that the lightest touch lit up her body. She tried not to succumb to it and mostly succeeded in her restraint; when she did give in, she redoubled her efforts to avoid it. What she felt was not worthy of the word love, it certainly did not condense into any sustainable emotion, but waned without leaving a trace, like a shooting star. She did not touch herself. Her body gradually withdrew from her. It shamed her like an animal, because she perceived her body and its needs as her real image. In order to fight this animal, she began to contradict her body, to tense a muscle instead of relaxing it, to hold in instead of letting go, to move counterintuitively, to lose touch with the primal and basic, until these unnatural gestures became second nature. She filled her days with sentences and ideas from ancient and modern literature. Her gestures also permeated into her reading, from which she took away nothing at all. The books affected the space around her, the comforting vowels and consonants that faded once she finished reading them. Her books did not inspire her with thoughts, but fortified the walls of her room and turned it into a home: the dark desk, the drawers with the brass knobs, the carpet of brown-black tones, the piano, her father's gramophone, the solid oak shelves mounted above her bed. That was where she had grounded herself and where she had first lost herself. She acceded to the words by way of imitation. A sentence that indicated a hand or mouth or body gesture led her to imitate it instinctively. Someone extended a hand, she followed suit. And when that happened, she did not question this marvel. She wanted the anonymous, immediate pleasure to cleave her like a sharp knife.

14

Elsa Weiss did not choose what to teach. She talked about everything apart from what truly concerned her. She was not dramatic; she neither breathed life into the subjects, nor went out of her way to interest or intrigue. It was the tyranny, which relieved the lessons of the dreary routine of grammar and syntax, of conversational English, that aroused interest. Only a single lesson resonated with a vibration that tyrannized us in a different manner. "Eveline." She pronounced the name of Joyce's story with something of a sigh or longing, protracting the transition between vowels. "She sat at the window watching the evening invade the avenue. Her head was leaned against the window curtains and in her nostrils was the odour of dusty cretonne. She was tired. [. . .] But in her new home, in a distant unknown country, it would not be like that. Then she would be married—she, Eveline. People would treat her with respect then. [. . .] Her time was running out but she continued to sit by the window, leaning her head against the window curtain, inhaling the odour of dusty cretonne. Down far in the avenue she could hear a street organ playing. She knew the air. Strange that it should come that very night to remind her of the promise to her mother, her promise to keep the home together as long as she could. [. . .] —'Eveline! Evvy!' He rushed beyond the barrier and called to her to follow. He was shouted at to go on but he still called to her. She set her white face to him, passive, like a helpless animal. Her eyes gave him no sign of love or farewell or recognition." Elsa Weiss's harsh gaze softened with embarrassment, directed at no one in particular.

15

For several years after she graduated from high school, she continued to carry the girl she had been like someone who would never grow up, a stillborn. It was difficult to determine whether she was fully aware of the magnitude of her actions or their implications. While she did believe her conduct was sound and sober, she could not help but notice the thin layer of indifference that sheeted her conflicted decisions, for which frankly, in hindsight, she could never fully account, just as she could not understand how, later in life, she had come into full being precisely when it seemed that the world around her and everyone else was gradually shrinking. To travel to Paris, to get married: here too she tensed and relaxed alternatingly, at her full discretion. She was the one who had urged Eric to marry her, only a few weeks after they met for the first time through a high-school friend the summer of graduation, already knowing she was leaving for a year. She remembered how she had studied his handsome profile and told herself she was going to marry him, all the while aware of both the arbitrariness and inevitability of her decision, which made him squirm in his seat before he came to his senses and realized that she was serious. Laura Christmastree, who lived in the adjacent room of the boarding house during her first few weeks in Paris, did not conceal her misgivings. "I don't understand. You're not describing who he is, what you talk about, what he means to you." They fell into the habit of crossing the garden and sitting at Au Petit Suisse on the corner of de Vaugirard and rue Corneille. "I'm not asking to push your buttons. I'm simply trying to understand why." "It has to do with home, my parents, my family." "That's not enough. You have to know more. It's your life. What about you?" "I have to get married." "Why?" "He loves me." "I'm sure he's in love with you." "Either I do it now, or I never will." This conversation saddened her, why was she making light of it? Was it because she had all the time in the world, or because of her impatience, directed inward with either humility or indifference? Why did she think this question didn't even need to be asked? Where did she muster this resignation from, when no one had made any demands or entrusted her with their expectations? It was of her own making. She had the faint sense that this was the only time when she could still afford to act without thinking, to be the less important beneficiary of her actions. Of course, she knew she could marry at a later time. She was also confident of her passion for men, a passion ignited and extinguished in the blink of an eye, and summoned another feeling to furnish her with pleasant intimacy, rational and long-lasting, an intimacy that wouldn't exasperate. The question of what she really needed or wanted had never even crossed her mind. The future was clear, almost too clear, and as to married life—dimly devoid of dreams.

The wedding date was set for a year after her return from Paris. The school gymnasium, cleared especially for the occasion, was split down the middle by the two families, who had never met socially: Eric's Zionist family, his friends from the labor Zionist youth movement, and Elsa's Neolog family along with remnants of her mother's Orthodox bloodline, who swallowed their pride and made an appearance. Her parents were concerned about the Zionists' vulgar boisterousness, whereas Eric, who reminded her of Jan in his attitude toward her family, resented the affected aesthetic presence of the Neolog world at their wedding, viewing it as a detached and all-consuming desire for assimilation. He was not worried about the wedding itself; the food lovingly prepared over the past seven days and the dozens of wine bottles would serve their purpose, and no one would ruin their day with pointless arguments, he assured her. Shortly before the guests' arrival, already clad in her pleated white dress, she shut herself in one of the classrooms and sobbed and sobbed, until she realized that she was being summoned to the chuppah; her mother's urgent cry reached her like a distant rumor, breaking the silence in which she had engulfed herself, Elsa, Elinka, where are you? Where did she go? She had to collect herself and make herself presentable, without anger or petulance, to put on perfume to distract people from her state; she felt as much a guest as all the others, and she succeeded, by God she succeeded, in fooling everyone and for fleeting moments even herself, the smile plastered on her face, her teeth flashing, she circled him seven times, with this ring I thee wed. Behold, you are consecrated to me. She was lightheaded. The music nullified all disputes, and as it often happened to her, it quashed her self-doubt and gradually filled the space in her head as she hummed the addictive, rhythmic Csárdás, carried aloft by the tune until the moment it came to a halt, hesitating whether to continue before ceasing to dither with a swift stomp that declared yes, despite everything, yes, just like that.

She settled with Eric into the apartment next to her parents, and began teaching French at the Hebrew high school. A year later the war broke out. In late August of 1940, following the negotiations between Romania and Hungary presided over by Nazi Germany, it was decided that Northern Transylvania would be returned to Hungary. Two weeks later the Hungarian army entered Kolozsvár. One flag was taken down, and another raised in its place.

Many felt that the Germans were about to win the war. And yet, in their building, the tension brought on by the changing of the guard elicited no more than the usual sigh of adjustment and feigned expressions of courteousness between them and their Gentile neighbors. War raged across the globe, but not in their home. In the first few months they sought only to shut off from the rest of the world, to sit in the safety of their apartments and wait for this murky tide to pass. In any case there was very little they were allowed to do. On the top floor lived Mr. Kristof, a World War I veteran, and his wife, Magda, the painter, a childless couple who had practically adopted little Elsa when she was born. During the long winter evenings they invited her to their apartment to watch the card games they played with friends at their *yeshiva of below*, as her father used to call it with a note of concern, and fatten her up with Madártej. Elsa kept to herself the fact that she had been given special permission to enter Magda's atelier, a narrow and dim hall by the living room lined with a carpet of dried paint that no one had bothered to remove; a majestic white canvas was perched against a regal three-legged easel made from beechwood, all prepared in her honor with explicit permission from Magda to use the oil paints however her heart desired, coat upon coat, which she smeared on with the elation of idleness.

At the point of Elsa's exhaustion, Magda would enter to observe her "creation," and immediately beckon Mr. Kristof over to feast his eyes on the painting. "Such talent, Elsa, already at your young age you paint modern, expressive, experimental, expressionist," Mr. Kristof rhapsodized. "Yes, yes," Magda concurred while clasping her hands, "you have such power, you have a force in your hands." She was aware that her gift was not that of accuracy or clear contours, but an ability to squirt out streams of color, to do something whose quality stemmed from its richness, density, and energy. On the ground floor of the building lived old Ivagda, a widow whose husband had passed away at a very young age, leaving her with two boys who left the house years ago and moved to Budapest. Ivagda worked as a beautician in the houses of affluent women, Christian and Jewish, "waging war," so she told Elsa, on "the insult of old age"—the wrinkles, the flab, everything a woman deemed offensive to smooth sensibilities. Ivagda claimed that women were not afraid of death lurking at their door, but that it was difficult for them to grasp life as a process or a state of formation, because change frightened them. "Change scares them, you know why? Because it disrupts the harmony," she said and looked at Elsa with scathing seriousness, her cheeks glistening from oils and strange spectacles perched on the bridge of her nose while she toiled over a concoction of eggs, avocado, yogurt, lemon, and olive oil destined to be smeared onto eager faces around town. How puzzling it was that such a creature, who lived in the shell of its body like an igloo, would be the bearer of the tidings of youth throughout Kolozsvár, as if this message needed to go through her by process of elimination, as if the bearer of tidings herself needed to submit her body, each time anew, to some radical initiation trial, almost farce-like, and yet Elsa understood from Ivagda that the changes life brings about always respond to the innate conservatism of those who fail to understand that wisdom has to do with memory, people who refuse to grow, who fear nature, who fear what might ultimately strip their face, expose, defeat and destroy it. And yet, my livelihood depends on just that, Ivagda concluded her argument and gave Elsa a gentle swat on her bottom. "So I cannot complain."

Since Elsa—who was now Elsa Weiss—and her father did not teach in the state education system, they were able to maintain their positions. Eric ran the family fabric store. Like other members of the Zionist movement, he viewed the events as a warning sign signaling a one-way street, and joined forces with Jan to implore her and her parents to immigrate. Her parents believed they had time to contemplate the matter, that rash decisions and radical changes must be avoided. They preferred to wait and see what the day would bring. Every day they repeated that sentence, which sustained them as if it were all a matter of patience, as if a hidden yet indisputable horizon stretched between one day and the next. They were exhausted. She was determined to stay by their side.

Gradually, fragmented news about the events in Eastern Europe started filtering in, about the armistice agreement in France and the legislation against the Jews. Elsa's correspondence with Anne and Madeleine, friends she had made at the humanities club in the Latin Quarter during her time in Paris, had petered out months ago, and her attempts to revive the communication had all failed. She wondered whether the postcards she sent had even reached their destination. Acquaintances who followed the BBC, whether directly or through friends, circumventing the bias of the Hungarian press, described the indescribable. Apart from the well-founded rumors about the yellow badge and the restrictions imposed on Jews in public spaces, they told of mass deportations and imprisonment in concentration camps, even though it was unclear where exactly the people were being deported to, or what became of the deportees. Her parents continued to bless their good fortune of having their Elsa back, as if that fact alone was enough to protect, at least her, from what was yet to come. To be honest, she had never seriously considered leaving Kolozsvár and distancing herself from her parents. Not because she shared their beliefs, but because her own never seemed firm enough for her to abandon or undermine them. Her parents were more important than any particular belief she could hold and fight for. And yet, she was unnerved when she witnessed her father lose his composure, his sudden fits of rage, the arguments he would stir up with a persistence she had never encountered in him before, so far removed from his gentle and agreeable nature. He did not think the persecution of Jews in France was a concession the French government needed to make to the Germans. It was exactly like what was happening around Hungary, he claimed, an infectious anti-Semitism that adopted every Nazi pretext to get rid of the Jews. The French police were the Nazi's executive force, not because these people had been indoctrinated and become Nazis themselves, or even pretended to be, but because they hated foreigners to begin with. Colleagues from school and members of the community disagreed with him. "Machiavellian collaboration," one of his friends defined the situation, no murderous intention or particular malice. An opportunistic, calculated attempt, and who knows, perhaps even ultimately effective, to prevent France from getting further involved in the war. Something inside her had dulled during these political conversations, the subject saturated with such oversimplification and helplessness, they might as well have been discussing sports, the holidays, or the weather. She let the silence take over her, and in a sense she embodied with her presence a kind of shared silence. Years later she thought that might have been the first time she came across that word, "collaborators," conduct that was talked about with a reserved tone as if it were some form of submission, or an act of adaptation in which one sought to insinuate himself, in some conniving manner, into the successful course of history, an achievement without an effort, without sacrifice, by virtue of complicity in another's crime. By choosing to accept the worldview someone else has placed before you, instead of standing up to it, you validate it; even if you haven't studied it in depth, you allow it to rule, but only in order to gain something from it. It is all about the wish to survive, she thought. Survival is temporarily identified with the image of the future itself, and you know you must join this future, and not fight against it, to contribute to it in order to somehow be spared of it. These were ideas Elsa kept to herself. She recognized the monstrosity of this possible choice, a choice which enraged her father, and at the same time she tried to see the collaboration from the point of view of those who chose it, who believed it was the better choice, who believed nothing was off limits to protect their loved ones. She tried to understand them as she understood those who disagreed with them ideologically. Deep down, she assumed the collaborators had more of a sense of humor than others. They probably knew they weren't perfect. And yet, she wondered whether there were things you must, under no circumstances, go along with. She wasn't sure where to begin this conversation.

She also kept to herself the ambivalence her marriage inspired in her, the agonizing hardship she experienced in sharing her life. She, who toiled over making unity her distinct merit, knew that her soul was split and that she was hanging onto the relationship with empty devotion, pinning her hopes and her indifference on the passage of time as the only force that might mend it with persuasion or acceptance. Could it be said that she too was complicit? Of course. She never sought to be a hero. But neither did she seek to be this miserable. All her decisions thus far released the scent of collaboration. To study, marry, remain in Hungary, try to convince herself that she had once lived, and let herself believe that time had passed and that she had no leeway, that as far as her own life was concerned her fate was in the hands of others, that was how she was built; if there was any heroism in her at all, it did not manifest in deflecting external circumstances but only her ability to think, her integrity, her humor.

Her collaboration in effect concealed a great force of refusal, a burning and destructive force that she tried with all her might to hide, since she feared she would have to pay too high a price for it. She could not afford to say no to them, because there would be no ending to it, it was a sweeping no that might undermine all their sacred beliefs, and also because she did not fully understand the source of her agnosticism, of her radical and hollow atheism—she was even willing to admit that much—that took over her, and left no stone unturned. There was an unimaginable irony to her, a gap or single stride always stretching from one stance to the other, a fretful search to escape the suffocation of the conclusive. No stance was ever a home. She was not Orthodox like Grandma Rosa, not a Neolog like her parents, and not a Zionist like Jan. Perhaps she was the paradoxical product of the three powerful belief systems that closed in on her, an adamant but elusive rejection of each one of them, which cracked the comprehensive solutions they presented her. She was actually averse to the sheer notion of a solution and did not seek an alternative one. She wished to let things run their course without her intervention. But alas, her irony knew no bounds and spread to each of her gestures. She could neither belong to something nor someone, and not because she yearned for the multiple, but because she would lose interest in the one, almost instantly. Why had she been attracted to Eric? He was probably less opinionated than most of the men around her. All those strong beliefs exhausted her, filled her with dreariness, but their absence also felt pallid. Her ambivalence made her panic, the recognition that she would never be able to decide, never be able to commit, which she could have attributed to her husband's passivity but knew was actually something inside her, something she only half-admitted to, that she was trying to hide from others and perhaps also from herself.

She began to sleep in her clothes, a thin, frayed plaid dress, thick stockings, and a wool sweater, in a separate room, a room designated as her study, whose windows she and Eric had sealed with tape back when the city was being bombed, and since then hadn't opened. During sleepless nights, she thought about those people she had met in Paris only a few years before the worst had befallen them, before their world fell apart. She tried to recall, one by one, the details from her time with them, details she might not have noticed then, while engaged in routine conversation; she tried to conjure up what they looked like, to see whether there was something suspicious or abnormal in the atmosphere that she had failed to detect. But what could she have actually done? She agonized over the fact that she never stepped outside of herself, that she lacked the ability to step outside of herself. She waited impatiently for daybreak. The breakfasts she prepared for herself and Eric, before they left for work, were eaten in silence. They didn't talk about what was going on between them. On rare occasions, they lashed out at each other. Together, with sincerity, even tenderness, they worked to preserve a semblance of normalcy. They could not afford to separate.

16

In the seventies, the principal, Mr. Ben Ami, a gaunt and miserly history teacher, a pince-nez permanently wedged on the bridge of his hooked nose, embodied the centralized power at school. During recess he would stand in the stairwell, one hand occasionally reaching for the white, meticulously pressed handkerchief in the breast pocket of his gray suit, his other extended to pull in the parade of students with an insistent shake of his fist. He kept them in close proximity for a long, painful moment to inquire about their studies; then he loosened his grip and with it the anonymous power of his authority, which left no lasting impression on anyone.

The decision to appoint him principal astonished Elsa Weiss. She had never been particularly interested in the politics of the school board, but unlike the supervisors or inspection committees that came and went, this case invaded her everyday life. Her heart was filled with foreboding. From the very first moment his appointment was announced at the teachers' meeting, she grumbled that it was a mistake and that he would work to bring her down. "He wouldn't dare mess with you, he only bullies the weak," Miss Alon, the civics teacher, tried to alleviate her concerns. But in this case, Weiss proved to be right. The first few months went by nearly without a hitch, apart from the opening session of the school year. Ben Ami had been a member of the Betar Movement back in Poland. He left behind his family, later killed in the Holocaust, immigrated to Israel and enlisted in the ranks of the Etzel. The details of his actions during that period were locked and sealed and imbued him with the glow of a warrior, which he preferred to call "glory," following his revered teacher and mentor, Zeev Jabotinsky. The word glory was inserted every so often into the speech he gave at the festive teachers' meeting held before Rosh Hashanah. Weiss rarely attended the meetings—"a waste of time"—but on the stenciled message placed in her locker the words "mandatory attendance" were printed in bold letters. "Unthinkable!" she grumbled. "Everyone should just do their own job." Nevertheless, she reported on the appointed day. "I am pleased to announce the commencement of the 1976 school year," Ben Ami declared. "Our school embodies the miraculous glory of Tel Aviv's higher education system." Weiss grimaced. "Idiot," she hissed to Miss Alon who was sitting, as usual, next to her. "Let it go, what is he to us? Principals are a dime a dozen, here today, gone tomorrow." "We must maintain our high standards," Ben Ami continued. "Our sons, as proven more than once, are the best and brightest, salt of the earth, *amor patriae nostra lex*." He couldn't help uttering the phrase in Latin, which he spoke—he made a point of informing his students and colleagues—fluently. "Salt of the vile Revisionists," Weiss mumbled to Miss Alon. "See how pompous he is? And he has a grudge against me." Miss Alon looked at her quizzically, as if to ask what could possibly have happened between them. Weiss indeed wondered long ago whether she might in fact know him from somewhere; they couldn't have met before, they had not passed through the same places, either here or in Europe; and yet she felt as though they had met before, or maybe he was simply a type. She tried to alleviate the tension his particular presence stirred in her, the kind that got under her skin, that embodied all the fanaticisms she found so utterly intolerable. Mr. Ben Ami tapped his fingers on the table in order to silence the din of unrest in the room, and augment the impression of his words. "Last year our finest boys enlisted in the most elite units . . ." She knew he wrote for *Herut* during the fifties—who had told her that? Perhaps Jan, she could no longer remember—and she could sense his dislike of her. Her doubtful, ironic gaze unnerved him. He must have wished her gone, replaced with a younger, more submissive teacher. "Well, you don't exactly like him either, what do you care what he says? The man is such a weakling he probably can't even hold a cap gun," Miss Alon tsk-tsked in her ear. "Those are the most dangerous ones." "In the upcoming year we will take our students on day trips to the battle sites of 1948. And in keeping with our school's glorious tradition, the senior trip will be to Shavei Tzion, where we will debate questions that touch the very core of our existence, and I expect the full attendance of the faculty, not only the homeroom teachers. The importance of participation cannot be overstated." A groan traveled between the walls. "A servant when he reigneth," Miss Volach was heard whispering to the geography teacher. "We'll cross that bridge when we come to it," Miss Alon now mumbled. "It can be overstated," Weiss's voice blared. "What?" "You heard me. The importance of participation can be overstated, and this is overstating. Sending the homeroom teachers, *soit.* So be it. But we've never joined the school trips before and there is no reason to change things now." "It is important the students know that we are of one mind on fundamental issues." "But we are not of one mind and there is no we," Weiss said, and began to gather her belongings. The meeting was already about to end. Ben Ami shot her a harsh look, as if to say—this isn't over. Clearly, they had started on the wrong foot. "Eventually he'll be interfering with the material we teach," Weiss said to Alon once they left the teacher's lounge. "Maybe with the young teachers, but not with the senior ones. Just wait, he'll calm down." Ben Ami had decided to assemble all students for bi-weekly lectures, to which he invited "superior individuals from all walks of life," industrialists, rabbis (*laborare est orare*, Weiss scoffed), military officers, physicians and writers. Ms. Weiss overcame her reclusive inclinations only when attending the concerts his deputy, Vice Principal Berkowitz, organized during Tuesday lunch recess. However, Ben Ami's influence had already begun to crack the shell of her routine. She felt as though he was stalking her, seeking an opportunity to say something reserved for her alone. Even she was astonished to see how ultimately fragile her routine was.

One day, while leaving the classroom to go down to the yard, as was her custom, she ran into him, standing in her path and blocking her way. Before she could greet him with a curt hello, he hissed at her: "You're behaving like a Nazi." For a moment she didn't understand what he wanted. Then she raised her arm with a swift movement, pushed him away, and rushed off.

Those words, Holocaust, SS, kapo, Nazis, were on everyone's lips. They were tossed around every which way, worn out, inundated with a vapidness when used in response to any manifestation of insensitivity, indifference to suffering or senseless cruelty. They said "Nazi" not to call things as they were, but because many things simply lacked the proper names. Like always, the names were late to come, they did not fit the phenomena—neither the names for public ailments nor for private illnesses, and certainly not those that sought to give expression to the connections between them. That which had no name did not exist. A few years later—but already about a decade after Elsa Weiss passed away—a pseudo-intimate language was formed, consensual and self-assured, one that articulated the mental history of the individual with greater accuracy and dealt with pathologies openly, in a manner that allowed for intervention and the acceptance of responsibility. Depression and melancholy, anorexia and bulimia were spoken about frankly, people were sent to psychotherapy and family counseling, and were even hospitalized when necessary. But at the time the public sphere was still very much taken up with taboos. The invention of names had yet to catch up.

In that crack between the distress and the absence of names she approached me, only once. Until then our relationship had been matter-of-fact and mutually respectful. In the course of the very first year, when she passed between the rows to hand back papers, she said to me, "You know English." "I took private lessons," I replied. Her gaze lingered on my eyes. It wasn't love. It was the modest affection a teacher might feel for her students. I didn't dream that she would gather me into her lap, I didn't imagine the touch of her hand. She was a lapless teacher, a teacher who did not grant patronage. She treated me like a mother superior who recognized the progress of her exemplary pupil, approving her conduct with a nod and without developing a personal relationship with her, without fanning the flames of her love. I did not always want her to notice me. At times I sought her validation, and at other times I wanted to be invisible in the classroom, to get through the lesson in one piece. In that incident, she summoned me to the blackboard. During that period I had already closed myself off inside a cell that diminished my size, a cell that imprisoned my youth. I shed pounds and more pounds without realizing what was happening to me. I imagined myself without body, and waged a mighty war against my voracious appetite. Weiss stood up straight and let her hand wander slightly, her fingers brushing against the hem of my pants, which hung humiliatingly slack around my emaciated leg. "What's going on with you?" she asked. "Are you okay?" She wasn't making fun of me. She wasn't putting me on display. Even though my back was to the class and my face to the blackboard, even though all eyes were on us, it was a private moment, our moment, whispered to me behind my back, to my ears only, a moment in which her heart went out to me, from behind, not head on. I was embarrassed. I did not look at her. I turned around and went back to my seat. I knew she would remember, I knew she knew and saw; I did not know what she knew and saw. It seemed the only intimacy that was possible was an intimacy from an infinite distance, an ephemeral covenant made behind my back, lacking the ability to rescue either of us from ourselves or from her loneliness.

The "Nazi" that burst out spontaneously from the principal's mouth could have been, simply, innocuously, a metaphorical provocation, even if it had the potential of becoming serious. But its malicious, intentional use was of course an entirely different matter. It had, this use, precedents. He knew it and she knew it, and as far as both were concerned, at least with regard to historical consciousness, which presumably linked them, it was tantamount to a court conviction. She did not think she needed to explain to him why that was. What did he really want from her? Did her arbitrariness threaten his tyranny? Or perhaps he wanted to test her weak spot, to see what his adversary was made of? In ancient or medieval history, she might have been charged with heresy or witchcraft. Even if she had thought him resentful and hard-hearted, she had not thought him capable of this. This was sheer spite. The greatest insults have a way of resonating throughout a school. There is nothing like the insults hurled at us when we wish to learn or teach. They are equivalent to the insults of love, because they too pertain to self-love.

She could not move on as if nothing had happened. She would no longer exchange a single word with him. All the reconciliatory gestures and good will the other teachers enlisted in an attempt to mediate were futile. The inability to make peace had led her into an all-out war, first and foremost with herself. Nothing was as it once had been. She saw him everywhere, hairy, thin, ugly, humped, diabolical, condemning and wreaking havoc, standing on every staircase landing, following her with his withering gaze, siccing his agents on her all around town. She heard his astringent, squeaky voice in others who wished her ill, in students who sat in class with half-buttoned shirts and considered her with impudent and brazen looks. When she entered the classroom, she suspected he had installed bugging devices in her absence, and when she was at home, hidden eyes followed her from inside the walls. Harbingers of evil surrounded her.

Wherever she turned she saw the distorted face of ridicule, and inside her the face of bitterness formed, the face she had always tried to escape. It was as if she had no face, as if her face was no longer her own. For the first time in her life she felt defeated, that she had nothing more to say to them, nothing, not in Hebrew and not in English. If back then that choice, an English teacher, had made perfect sense, the logic of a neutral language, the language of no one, the unsullied language of no one beloved, if she had once fought, through the language of empiricism and hard facts, the language of skepticism and irony, to form a shared vocabulary and lucid rules of grammar that would enable a sane world of fair exchange between her and her students—now that logic was lost on her, and the battle had abandoned her. Hopeless, she saw only the holes in the web she had spun. Her old force flinched from her like a foreign body. Everything she did to alleviate the burden only weakened her further. She fumbled over her words. She knew she still sounded clear, intelligible, but she felt it was only a matter of time before she would be exposed. She had no desire to make an effort. She did not want to listen, could not listen. She no longer wanted to speak in any language.

17

She goes to kindergarten and learns to swear in Romanian and Hungarian. She can't understand why the language of the hostile neighbors arouses the gravitational pull of swear words, because Jan claims there is no comparing Romanian curses to their Hungarian ones, and that if the *seggfejek* that run this country were also human beings, he might consider being a patriot and staying here. She is mesmerized by her spontaneous outpour and by the useful talisman deposited in her small, unpracticed hands, enabling her to hurl these precious profanities at whomever she perceives as weak or inferior to her, whomever she thinks will not be able to repay her in her own currency, because her words will render him dumbfounded, as if she has cast a spell on him. Years later, as a teenager, she herself would turn into the object of that spell's force. Time after time, words would bring her to tears. A friend in high school would describe to her the dubious trade, as she insisted on putting it, of a wayward acquaintance of her parents. "And you know what she does with those young guys she teaches in her living room?" "What?" Elsa asks, failing to understand. "She fucks them. Why are you crying? What's wrong with you? There's no talking to you anymore." But in kindergarten she juggles these dirty words as if playing with a ball, rushes home and swears at their maid, and Jan hears it from his room and becomes enraged and demands that she apologize at once. She remembers the horrible shame that gripped her, how she ignored the maid's eyes welling up with tears because of what she herself had created with her words, how she slouched along with Mother and Jan to the maid's house later that night to ask her forgiveness, in that sane world in which they at least attempted, even under less mystical notions than her own, to strive toward harmony between the words and the situations, to pacify and compensate precisely because not everything could be said or done with arbitrariness.

18

Ten-year-old Moshe, Sarah's twin brother, is leaning against the side of the barrack and trying to catch his breath. He's watching in utter terror as the children close in on him in a half-circle. It takes Elsa, who has just entered the makeshift classroom in the corner—on nicer days she teaches in the open air—only a second to realize they are playing Mr. Cohen's scandal, which sent the camp into a frenzy last night after he was once again caught stealing bread from the women's barracks. The entire morning she tried to fight off the suffocating heaviness in her chest since being awoken at around two in the morning by the sound of bare feet fumbling toward Mrs. Farkash's bunk, where the latter had hidden leftovers in case one of her two children woke up hungry. She knew what would happen once Mr. Cohen got his hands on the bread. The women who were light sleepers would cry out, the children would run to summon the men in the nearby barrack and pandemonium would break loose. Mr. Cohen, who resembled a gray and pockmarked punching bag waiting to be swung at, probably knew that at no hour of the day was it truly possible to steal, even when darkness descended and people were forced to close their eyes. She caught his gaze for a split second, and it seemed to her as if this time, too, he had wished to be caught.

If she thought the children would take her mind off the adults' games, her hopes had gone up in smoke. She sits in the corner and grants them permission to continue playing with a slight nod. Eight-year-old Esther, unanimously chosen for the role of supervisor because her father is a lawyer, presides over the investigation with a sternness that does not suit her nature or her chubby, animated cheeks: "It can't go on like this." "But it wasn't me. I swear. You're making a horrible mistake. I'm being falsely accused. I'm a decent person, I have a family. You want to destroy me? That's what you want?" Esther tilts her head skeptically. "We all know it was you, Mr. Cohen. There's no point trying to hide it." Moshe's tiny, furrowed face flushes crimson, standing out against the sickly pallor of his friends; he raises a leg and kicks the air as if to keep them at bay, then retreats back into himself. "We won't get one word of truth out of him by being nice," Jano, standing about half a meter behind the others, blares impatiently. He is eleven, the oldest in the group. "You piece of shit," he turns to Moshe and draws closer to him. Moshe flinches in panic. He backs into the corner and fights to keep himself from bursting into tears. Sarah looks at Elsa nervously. She has been seeking her proximity from the very first day of school, when she took the rag she had brought with her, rolled it into a long tube, pressed it against her thick glasses, and sought out her teacher's gaze. "How do I look through your telescope? Am I photogenic through the hole, Sarah?" Elsa had asked, signaling that she remembered the girl's name, and wresting a smile from her permanently worried face. With her pudgy body and slightly ungainly gestures, the girl rushed to greet her every morning before roll call. She ran up to her simply to feel her presence, fumbling on the ground for objects people had dropped at random in order to bring them to her, her mouth agape as if struggling to say something while at the same time making sure nothing would escape it. Moshe tattled on her mockingly a few days ago that even in her sleep she mumbles, "Miss Elsa, oh, Miss Elsa." Sarah glared at him and denied with tears, "I do not! You're just making it up." "I'm not making it up at all. Mother says you have an obsheshion with Miss Elsa." "*Obsession*," Elsa corrected him and smiled. "I was also obsessed with my teachers." Sarah looked at her despondently, as if trying to say that it wasn't the same thing, whereas Elsa remained silent and didn't tell her how she too as a child felt that her Torah teacher was coursing through her veins, and how she feared she was insulting her mother with the love she had for someone else, even though her mother never even noticed. That she too had imagined at the time that something infinitely important was happening in her teacher's life, and thought that if only she had been given the opportunity she could have helped her, could have comforted her in her loneliness, so she wouldn't have to carry her secret alone.

Now Sarah is tilting her body forward and urging everyone to reconcile. "What are you suggesting? That we ignore it again? That we let him keep on stealing because under such conditions stealing is no longer an offence?" Jano is losing his patience. "You selfish lowlife, you piece of shit," he raves, "scum of the earth, that's what you are." Elsa wonders whether she should let this scene turn into a brawl. Until now she has chosen to remain silent. "Maybe you could teach us how to swear in English and French?" Herman asks, as if reading her thoughts. "So we could

78

curse the gendarmes and the guards." "And the SS-ka from morning roll call," Esther chirps, "so they won't be able to understand what we're saying." They turn to her mischievously. "You must be careful with swear words. People hear them first. *C'est le ton qui fait la musique*. It's the tone that makes the music.

19

The relative safety, perhaps the instinctive complacency, that the Weiss, Bloom, and other families around them felt during the first years of the war, collapsed all at once in March of 1944, after the German invasion of Hungary and the transformation of Kolozsvár, two months later, into a ghetto on the outskirts of town, with between ten and twenty thousand inhabitants—she read this estimation in a book years later, although the vague figure indicated nothing more than the chaos their lives had become. If once every minor change or random deviation from her routine was enough to evoke restlessness, the utter disarray now peeled off the protective layers she was accustomed to and prompted her to seek new ones. The yellow badge, which she and Mother had measured meticulously, ten centimeters in diameter, and stitched onto the left side of their jackets in the style of a uniform, caused her both distress and, paradoxically, comfort, because once the badge was removed—and she had no doubt it would be—it would signal the end of the reign of terror, and life would resume its normal course. What she had once called, not without criticism, a voluntary ghetto—those crammed, dim streets, in her child's eyes, which snaked between the synagogue, the butcher, the baker, the fish sellers, and cheders, that reeking city-inside-a-city miles away from the theaters, the cinema, the churches, the cathedral, and the university she loved so much, a city-inside-a-city that did not lack *joie de vivre* but nevertheless always made her recoil in suspicion—was now her reality. As if she had been forced to return to some kind of primal nature, to the noise of the definitive identity she had always found so intolerable and refrained from displaying, even if she did not exactly wish to hide from it. Almost everyone had stumbled in this delicate dance even before the war. While the few neighbors still alive in their building were devastated by the news of their departure (old Ivagda had passed away back in '43, and Mr. and Mrs. Kristof had aged significantly over the years and barely left their apartment; Elsa used to help them with their shopping), most Hungarians in Kolozsvár were indifferent to what was happening around them; but she did not interpret this indifference as cold-heartedness or disdain for the Jews. She thought that what was happening didn't threaten them directly, and that they were determined to preserve their daily routines just as she and the others had clung to their habits only a few months earlier, after reading in the papers about the calamity that had befallen others both distant and near, even right by their border.

Now she heard about anti-Semitic incidents on a daily basis, about people around them—acquaintances whose names she knew, passersby whose existence she noticed—who were suddenly taken away, arbitrarily, to a concentration camp. Of course it could happen to them as well, it was impossible to deny the reality that something awful was going on, and her thoughts sometimes mixed with a wish that she be relieved already of something she was ill-suited for. Once, before the announcement in early May expelling the Jews to the ghetto, she went for a stroll around town alone, without wearing the badge, as if challenging the regulations that explicitly prohibited leaving one's apartment not only at night but during most hours of the day. The city was silent and deserted; even in the commercial areas the weariness was felt. She rushed past the pool—pretending not to notice the sign on the front door printed in black letters, "No Entry for Jews"—in order to get to the park, which also wasn't overrun with people, unlike regular days during early afternoon hours, making her wonder whether the changes had already reached what seemed to her the other side of the world. She sat on a bench at the edge of the park as if considering whether to enter, and was suddenly gripped by the odd urge to share something about herself with another girl who sat on another bench, also alone, not far from her, to tell her that while she was wandering around in broad daylight, she was actually doing it covertly, but something stopped her, blunt gestures were not in her nature, or perhaps it was merely the fear that she would be incriminating herself. She lingered there for a while, contemplating what to do next, and then decided to open the book she had with her, *Nausea* by Sartre, but didn't really read it, only skimmed the pages, and for a moment felt overcome by fatigue, not from a lack of alertness, but a kind of internal desire to detach; and then she thought perhaps it wasn't a very good idea to come here, she wasn't able to derive a shred of pleasure from it, but she could have anticipated that. In a parting gesture, she smiled as if telling herself a joke, a gesture that even had a certain theatricality to it, to tread the same paths, to sit on the same bench, to open a book as she had in the past, to observe her surroundings with the same distracted gaze. She took a deep breath, almost relaxed, and considered going to the nearby café to order a hot chocolate and Dobos torte for old time's sake. This thought also amused her, and she once again gazed across the park; but the houses and figures gradually distanced themselves as if withdrawing from her, the sky grew dark, and she had to get up and leave. She stood up hesitantly, but when realizing it would indeed be for the last time, she shook herself and glanced around again, to make sure she was safe and no one was looking at her, and she turned back home, struggling not to break into a run and arouse suspicion. Eric stared at her at the entrance helplessly. "Are you mad? Do you have any idea how worried we were?" She curled up in the corner of the living room couch and held her head between her hands. Then she looked up at him. "I'm sorry," she said. "I shouldn't have done it. I apologize." "You have no idea," he said with a weary expression.

Things went downhill at a dizzying pace. The dispossessions, the confiscations, the freezing of bank accounts, the burning of books by Jewish authors, the arrests on the street. Until then, her Jewish identity hadn't told her anything meaningful about herself, and it seemed odd to her that the identity a person was randomly born with could turn into the subject of shame or pride. Not only because she usually felt comfortable around non-Jews, but because she could not ascribe a general attitude or shared consciousness to the community. In Paris, she and a young American girl her age who had lived in the same boardinghouse, she couldn't remember her name, had taken a walk together one day to the Jewish Quarter. She had approached Elsa and asked to join her, and Elsa said why not, gladly, and they strolled along the bank and passed the Notre-Dame and crossed Pont Marie and the Ile Saint-Louis and walked down rue Pavée to rue des Rosiers, where Elsa decided to enter a shop of Judaica and sacred books.

She perused the books for a while, as if meeting an old acquaintance, and when they left the young American told her she felt suffocated, that they must leave the Quarter at once, and looked at her with fresh eyes as if suddenly seeing something intimidating in her, something unbearable. What was that thing, what had she seemingly discovered about her? What did she suspect her of? Elsa did not confront her, and perhaps did not even consciously ask herself these questions, and they returned to the boarding-house in silence and no longer sat together; in fact, they never exchanged another word. She did not feel distress because she had not become attached to that woman, but recalling the incident now, she realized she had instantly dismissed what had happened, had rushed to shrink its dimensions to a mere accident. She is Jewish. But she refuses to make an issue of it. She could fill it with substance, but she doesn't want to. She has a different world and she's happy within it. Now she wondered what other things she had ignored, what else she had averted her gaze from. Because there were, of course, other incidents she did not understand, or simply refused to understand, for example the wonderment of that woman whom Elsa rushed to help with her suitcase all the way up to the train station, and when the woman asked for Elsa's name and Elsa replied, she responded with bafflement: "Jewish?" as if something in her behavior, a Jewish girl lending her, a Christian, a hand, was an obtuse breach of the natural order, ultimately causing more embarrassment than good.

They took only a few belongings upon their forced move to the ghetto, established in the Iris brick factory on the outskirts of Kolozsvár, mainly sheets and blankets, used alternatingly for covering the dusty floors and serving as makeshift partitions between the families, in the absence of walls, in order to maintain a semblance of privacy. They did not need more blankets, the summer still in full swing. In the days prior to the move, since losing their jobs, they spoke little to each other. She could not remember what was said, only the emptiness of the masking words that took over their conversation during those long hours in which they waited for the arrival of the gendarmes. She filled her bag with keepsakes and a few books, which she believed no one would covet and seize. The heavy furniture, the paintings, the libraries, the gramophone, and piano were reluctantly left in their apartments. A seal was immediately imprinted on the doors shut behind them—property of the Hungarian nation. She witnessed this as she was violently pushed with the others toward the truck covered in tarp, hurtling along the streets toward the ghetto. Did she already understand the implications? The crowdedness inside the barb-wired area, with the police officers and gendarmes, made the imposed restrictions on movement sound like a cruel and ridiculous joke, only that now she no longer allowed herself to make light of them.

There were no toilets. The pits that were dug for the men and women, which could serve twenty people at once, were almost completely exposed. Apart from the filth, the inconvenience and distress, she found it difficult to squat, even though she was limber, she feared she would lose her balance and fall, a thought that made her sway from side to side and forced her to place her fingertips on the ground to steady herself. She accompanied her mother to help her empty her bowels and later to wash herself with a bit of water, which was also rationed for cooking and drinking. She also joined her in the long lines for food, imploring her in vain to stay in her room to rest; she must go, she told her, she could not laze about like a caged lioness, she had to see with her own eyes the thieves doling out the rations, perhaps her admonishing glare would encourage them to abandon their deviant ways. For years there had hardly been any physical intimacy between her and her mother. Their hugs were awkward, even though she could not remember when exactly she had stopped curling up in her mother's arms and seeking the smell of her body. Her mother never exacted a price for this change, nor did she even attempt to account for it. Did she even sense it? Now she stood close to her helplessness, and memories of Grandma Rosa on her deathbed—Elsa was ten at the time—flitted before her, the old woman's eyes fixed on her mother as if telling her, You are the strong one, I am the weak one, and the voices that preceded (but did such a conversation ever really take place?), "I don't want to be a burden." "You are not a burden." And she remembered herself thinking, Mother, don't say that, tell her something else. But how could it be said differently? Tell her that you need her. That hasn't been true in a long time. What does it matter? Elsa began to cry, she was a weepy child, but at about twenty years of age, when she stopped crying, the sound of wailing rose around her, bone-chilling howls that tore through the sky, and she wondered if even in the maternity ward the women's cries were replacing the cry reserved for her and her baby.

During that period rumors of deportation started to circulate; they said there was a very real possibility that their lives were in danger. Eric, who maintained frequent contact with the representatives of the youth movements, cautiously shared these warnings with her, partly disbelieving the words that left his mouth, partly fearing her response. It was not a concentration camp in which people were put to work, but an extermination camp, with incinerators. She listened with the same skepticism she had applied to his "exaggerations." Not because she did not want to know the truth. On the contrary, she preferred the truth, she assured him, any truth, but she could not be expected to believe unreliable fragments of information clouded by ideological motives. She was not particularly fond of those Zionists, thought them deranged, fanatics, vain, assuming authority that did not belong to them and stirring up panic, mainly among older people too helpless to oppose them. "What do you want them to do?" she asked, enraged. He told her that he had heard things around the ghetto from refugees from Slovakia, Yugoslavia, and Poland, people who had lost jobs, homes, families, who had lost everything and were now seeking shelter here, attempting to falsify identification cards. "Do you realize what's happening?" "Are you sure you understood them? They don't speak Hungarian or German or Romanian. Why do you think the Jews of Poland and the Jews of Hungary share the same fate?" During these rancorous arguments she would whip out the expression "a Hungarian of the Mosaic faith" without the least bit of sarcasm. Rolling her eyes, and with what humor she had left, she skillfully recited the glorious Jewish past, as taught in the Neolog school—their role in the "golden age," in the social elite, in the parliament, in literature, medicine, architecture. And in "the weapons and steel industry," he chimed in. They burst into laughter. "And don't forget that Horthy's mother-in-law is Jewish!"

In hindsight, she could liken the small, quiet dinners they had with her parents to sitting among the critically ill, but lacking the comfort that organic processes sometimes provide, if only because the source of the tragedy was bound up with one's physical state and beyond human control. Moreover, they were not ill, her parents, only slightly weakened, but "thank God, healthy," an expression that escaped from her mouth only with regard to them. The combativeness that characterized her father in the early days of the war had deserted him, replaced by a helplessness that crystalized in the look he gave her at their moment of parting, the kind she had only seen in paintings of purgatory, a look in which horror and panic coalesced with infinite distance.

It was during one of these dinners that she first heard about the possibility of a rescue train to Palestine. Eric did not present it alone; he enlisted an old friend of her parents, Dr. Tibor Müllner, a distinguished judge who used to join them for cholent on Shabbat when she was a girl and sabotaged "the conversation's free flow of ideas"—as Jan complained bitterly afterward—by pontificating about the intrusive effect on the digestive system of the white beans with smoked goose, a speech that must have utterly exhausted him given the fact that immediately upon finishing the main dish, even before the compote was served, he would enter her room without seeking permission and sink into his afternoon nap, leaving the rest of the guests speechless. Müllner, who was a close acquaintance of Jóska Fischer's, said that while they could not fight the Germans with force, that did not mean there weren't other ways to save Jews, since Germany was indeed losing its power, with the allies at their doorstep. Hopefully, Germany would soon be defeated. They must try to buy time and hold out, and meanwhile try to save as many Jews as possible. They could try to escape and hide out in Romania or Yugoslavia, but it was dangerous and it certainly could not become a collective tactic; the Hungarian newspapers were publishing frightening articles cautioning against escape and threatening to put to death anyone caught at the border. Her father suddenly exclaimed: "Escape? But that's against the law!" She remembered the shock that washed over the faces of the two other men: "Bloom, apparently you're failing to understand our reality." He had no guile, and neither did she. It took time for her to learn suspicion, and even when she did, it remained an external layer like the heavy makeup she would come to apply years later. Müllner reiterated that a mass escape from Hungary was not a possibility. A few might try, and even succeed. However, and here he was approaching the heart of the matter, the Germans could be bribed. "But if it's about to end," her father said, "if it's a matter of mere weeks, perhaps we had better wait it out?" "They might take the extreme action of someone who has nothing to lose," Müllner stressed, "but on the other hand it seems they have a lot to lose, and perhaps they can still lose less, and that is exactly why we must try to negotiate with them, to discover their weakness." "Would it not be better to reach out to the Hungarian authorities?" "They refuse to have any contact with Jewish representatives. And do remember it's the Hungarian gendarmes who have been putting the Jews on the deportation trains recently. All the more reason we need to make it look like a deportation for the Hungarian authorities, put the Jews on the same cattle cars, since they might view any operation or rescue deal with the Germans as a betrayal. Our only way out is to negotiate with the Germans and no one else, and try to save as many people as we can."

The following conversations were not made in her presence. They must have been more specific. She understood from Eric that her father showed a reluctance toward the suggestion, that he had "more questions than a pomegranate has seeds," as Eric described it with a certain impatience. It was clear that he and Mother preferred to remain in Kolozsvár and send her off with Eric to reunite with Jan. "But how can I trust this Kastner character and put

Elsa on some train?" her father asked his son-in-law. "You have to understand," Eric replied, "that such a negotiation, devised behind closed doors, is built upon lies and pretenses. You couldn't have stomached it, let alone carried it out. I'm afraid I couldn't have either. But he can. It's a fact." "But what if he's lying to me too? How can I believe him?" "He has good intentions. I trust him. These days, he's the only one looking out for us. Take into account that he's also sending some of his own family members. You know them, they live a few blocks away . . ." "Maybe I didn't explain myself," her father said, "my problem isn't Kastner. It's the Germans I'm afraid of. It looks like a ruse. What do they have to gain from this? What do they need the Jews' small change? Who would even be interested in a group of women, children, and old men who could be of no use to anyone? I have a bad feeling that this is blackmail and the people who might thwart the initiative are certain Germans who don't like the idea that other Germans are in contact with the Jews. It goes against the very essence of the Nuremberg Laws. Even a stubborn Jew like myself knows this much." Eric agreed that it was a very bold gamble. "It may very well only draw out the inevitable, that we're all doomed no matter what. But at least someone is trying to act against what looks like an arbitrary blow of fate."

He tried to glean more information from Eric and Müllner, to find out who was preparing the passenger list, what the criteria were. He heard rumors of thousands of Jews storming the Aid and Rescue Committee offices, attempting to twist their arms, asking who had given them the moral right to make these decisions. "It isn't the committee members' right," Müllner replied, "it's their moral duty." "So be it." He did not know what to make of it. A cross-section of the community would be chosen, he was told, it seemed to be the most logical approach under the circumstances, but some people were buying their place with money and valuables.

He could not be persuaded to go. Years later, she would be amazed when she recalled how the three of them, her mother, her father, and she herself, clung to the humble apartments they had left behind in Kolozsvár, as if there was still a possibility they might return to them someday. He simply did not believe any harm would come to her if she stayed, only growing hesitant over time, when he realized he could not protect her.

When he asked to speak with her in private, she more or less already knew what he was going to say. He hadn't negotiated. It was important she know that. He had obtained certain privileges during his six years as school principal. He and Mother had decided to give their spots to her and Eric. He knew she was not happy in her marriage. He was sorry for that and hoped one day she would come to feel differently. He never told her what to do. He had given her advice, which she was entitled to accept or reject. Now she was an adult, and as such was allowed to give him advice in return. But on this matter he was still unequivocally a father to a daughter, perhaps even a father to a child. "Had I known," he said, "had anyone told me I was bringing my child into a world in which people behaved like this, I assure you I would never have had you." She asked for time to think about it. He told her there was no time. "This is not something one needs to prepare for. Pack what few possessions you may take, follow the orders." "But what kind of daughter would I be, what kind of child, if I left you at such a time?" "You're right," he replied and smiled. "The kind of daughter every parent dreams of having, the child you never were, the obedient child who does what her parents expect her to do. The child who understands I'm doing what she would have done with children of her own."

Among those climbing into the truck in the ghetto, which was headed to the Columbus Street Camp in Budapest, she spotted Clara and her mother. She was only superficially acquainted with the other town residents gathered there. They were asked to bring along a suitcase and provisions for ten days: two changes of clothing—summer clothes, as they were traveling to Palestine through Spain—six pairs of underwear, a plate, a spoon, a cup and a little canned food. They waited in Columbus for several days, maybe more. Every day more people showed up, fought with the guards at the entrance, asked who was in charge, they had to get on the train, they would not budge until they were let in, and waited for the guards' shift change, perhaps they could still find a way in. She had brought along books for the road, and tried reading while at the camp, but couldn't; what had she been thinking? And yet, for how long could she stand this idleness? This word, which her father used to criticize her innate absentmindedness, amused her now that she had ample time for idleness yet lacked the means for it; even idleness required certain favorable conditions. The presence of children and babies soothed her somewhat, not on the immediate level, of course, they screamed and would not relent, their parents could not explain even to themselves what exactly they were doing there and where they were heading, and there were children from the orphanage who seemed almost unresponsive, but she made a utilitarian calculation—which in all likelihood made sense nowhere but in her own head—and reached the conclusion that if there were children around, it probably wouldn't take much longer. The cigarettes that appeared in everyone's hands brought on a barrage of coughs. "How about putting out that cigarette? My child's asthmatic." "Fine." And yet another man stubbed out his cigarette with his thumb and placed the humiliated butt in his pocket. And one day, she couldn't tell how many days later, SS men came and led them through Budapest to the train station. They passed through these streets, familiar to some, with a new gait, the gait of someone who knows that very soon he is about to leave for good, and so walks hesitantly, as if to a clandestine funeral. It was the largest group she had ever marched with, bigger than the school or youth movement parades; what did she feel as she marched in step, did she notice the aversion, the suspicion, the disdain, did she encounter the hatred? What she sensed was that distant, elusive, almost apologetic gaze of those who were averse to atrocities taking place under their noses, not because they questioned the guilt of those paraded before them, but because they didn't want to know, didn't want to see, didn't want anything to do with it. And then, after a long hour, when she was already exhausted, she thought she saw her father also crossing the street; she was certain it was him, turned her head and called out to him, wanted to run to him. "Wait a second," she said, and attempted to escape the procession. You're mad, it's impossible, he's in Kolozsvár, you're dreaming. She knew it couldn't be.

The suitcases and food were unloaded upon their arrival and placed in the last cars. On July 1st, at one-thirty in the morning, the train departed. It carried nine hundred seventy-two women, seven hundred twelve men, and two hundred fifty-two children. As they pulled away from the outskirts of Budapest, the flashes of the bombings lit up the heavy darkness.

20

She folded her arms under her chest and pressed them into her ribs, while massaging her waist with her hands and swaying back and forth, as if seeking to alleviate the frequent shivers that wracked her body. For hours she struggled not to sit on the dry straw sheeting of the cattle car floor until she finally yielded, no longer able to stand on her feet. People alternately stood up and crouched. Eric implored her to try and sleep, afterward she could stand if she wanted, but first she must regain her strength. He fashioned a low bunk out of handbags, piled one of the blankets on top of it and spread the other over her knees, bending toward her and placing his wide hand on her feet, which had turned stiff with cold despite the heavy heat. Her fingers were numb and drained of color. She rubbed them together vigorously, pressing them between her knees until she felt them relaxing. The filth, she signaled to him with her eyes, but he shrugged that there was no choice and she must let it go. The rattle of the train along the landscape of barracks raised gray dust that wiped out the existence of the cities and villages, as if they were traveling through a different Europe.

As the first night fell, she lowered her gaze to the ground and let it wander to the sides of the car, seeking a neutral, faceless space, where she could be alone with herself and close her eyes. The motion was misleading, making her feel as if she were standing in place. Her mind emptied of thoughts and assumed the shape of the car's metal panels, incapable of preserving any of the sights from the great distance already consumed. Her body shivered with sweat, she couldn't tell whether from the chill or the fear, and then she lurched forward to grab onto the waist of an older man standing not far from her, taking her back twenty years, to the entrance hall of her parents' apartment, where she hugged at length a friend of her father's who was wearing a gray suit similar to his own, before abashedly pulling away from him to the roaring laughter of the guests. Something inside her gave rise to the thought that she would never return home, something that preceded emotion, something almost practical that made her believe she could manage in difficult situations; she was not a strong woman, but she was strong enough for this, despite the fact that nothing in her previous life had prepared her for it, she could endure the unknown, she could carry it and weather anything it might impede, or thwart, or prevent. And perhaps she wouldn't manage, since she had never managed before, she would simply adapt, ostensibly, outwardly. She scanned the people around her to gauge who was resilient and who was not. In the pitch black of the car she could see that the little girl who had been standing close to her all this time was staring at her. Her fogged up glasses slid down her pinched nose. She wrinkled her nose and tilted her head back like a magician performing a trick of sliding her glasses back up without using her hand. Her mother cautioned her with a look. "Stop it," she whispered to her. "But my glasses keep slipping," the girl whined in despair. She had two siblings in the car, one of them looked close to her in age. Elsa searched the girl's eyes to acknowledge that she saw her, then turned her gaze toward the tip of her own nose in an attempt to achieve a cross-eyed look that would coax a smile out of the frightened face in front of her. She wasn't sure the girl was resilient.

The planes circling nearby muffled the blare of the train's horns and the whistle of its engine, competing with the passengers' own ruckus until night descended and their loud voices were replaced by a pesky murmur that pounded the moans and sobs into an indistinct mash. The noises of the night troubled her above all. They heralded a continuous stretch of torment from which there was no escape. "Are you from Kolozsvár?" she was asked, in an attempt to engage her in conversation. "Yes." She knew that because of the Kastner family the answer provoked a certain tension, and was not the same as saying I'm from Budapest, or from one of the provinces. She thought about other answers, but a greater constraint paralyzed her, a constraint that she tried not to view as a type of indifference. It wasn't that she didn't care what others thought of her. She didn't think herself better than them. She felt different from them. She did not expect to feel at home in a cattle car with eighty other people, and yet, her sense of otherness suddenly struck her as it never had before, precisely because she was trapped inside a crowd that had left everything behind, like her, at short notice, in civilian clothes with the stitched yellow badge, precisely because she was experiencing, perhaps for the first time in her life, a tragedy that did not befall her alone, that did not create a gulf between her and everyone else, but rather forced upon her the language of the many, and even if it felt false, it was still unrelenting in its accuracy. "Are you from Kolozsvár?" "Yes."

There was a finite number of places. Someone was inevitably taking someone else's spot. Which implied that someone could have taken hers. It didn't mean that the others were doomed, they would simply have to find their own way out, and they would, she told herself, she believed they would, or someone would come to their rescue, since in the past months people had stopped trying to act on their own. Don't torture yourself with delusions. She knew she could have given her place to someone else. It wasn't something she could or wanted to tell her father. Maybe he knew, maybe he didn't. Perhaps he wanted to reignite her survival instinct. You couldn't tell the person who brought you into this world that you had no more strength to carry on, that everything they cherished, everything everyone was fighting for, now more than ever before, you didn't reject, certainly not, but you also didn't desire. Now it was her duty to live for him, who had given her a gift that he had deemed priceless, who had, for the second time, given her life. She needed to muster the strength. "What do you do?" "Teach French," she replied curtly. It seemed as though her interlocutor expected her to return the question. But she remained silent; she stood out in her persistent silence. They would not let her be. "Are you alone?" "I'm with my husband." They didn't ask who was left behind. One brother in Palestine, immigrated before the war. She could not utter his name without smiling. When had she last heard from him?

It felt as though she had been awake for more than five days, her eyes open, chewing on her lip so that shouts wouldn't escape from her as they did from the others, falling asleep for brief moments only to wake up again, uncertain where she was and how long it had been since the train first departed. Had she been able to, she would have forgone sleep, simply to avoid the terrifying moment of waking. A heavyset woman, who shifted between standing and sitting beside her, moaned loudly right next to her ear. She couldn't say anything or try to silence her. They stopped every now and again for long breaks, to empty their bowels and stretch their legs. But the long hours inside the cars took their toll. The stench of urine and feces mixed with the smell of the provisions they had brought, cans of food either too salty or too spicy that left them parched and produced a collective acrid breath that filled the air, and like the noise, grew increasingly monotonous, like a viscous rot that at some point she stopped smelling. The crowdedness and darkness veiled the passengers' faces. Of course, most of them she had never met before. She remembered the conversation between Father and Müllner about the principle of allocating travel permits—political, social, and religious, they had said. It had a certain logic to it; she understood that logic. The portrait disassembled the public into atomized, allegedly essential components, and placed them side by side in the cramped space, like a cubist painting, in such a manner that prevented them from being reassembled back into a whole she could identify. Only later would she come to recognize what made them a whole. It was tucked into the twofold lesson etched onto their flesh. Without a moment's notice you could tear people away from the houses they had toiled their entire lives to build; you could feed them only enough not to perish; you could drag them through the unknown, pressed together in ways they had never thought possible; you could torment them in an unfamiliar space and before strangers; you could humiliate and demean them, and they would continue to stand on their feet. Only a few would collapse. Fewer still would commit suicide. The second lesson would be revealed when someone, no one knew who, mistakenly replaced the name of the Auspitz Station with Auschwitz. Word spread through the train like a plague, and until it proved to be a misunderstanding, it served to expose the convoluted nature of privilege, which could turn at any moment into a double-edged sword.

On the sixth day she awoke to the sound of hysterical screams. She was exhausted as if after a long run and could barely stand up straight. She heard they were being ordered to get off at Linz Station and would be led by foot to a military camp on the outskirts of town, for a shower. First she hesitated whether to hasten her steps or to squeeze to the back of the line, and then resolutely fended off the rumors and threats buzzing around her, quickly dragging Eric to the front of the line, as if the shower were a respite that could restore the humanity she had been robbed of. The sun stood in the middle of the sky and heavy beads of sweat trickled down her face. They had already caught up with the others and arrived at the place, but now the men and women were being separated, and she heard the older women say, this is it, we're finished, and the younger ones silenced them, because they were ordered to undress and hand over their bundle of clothes for disinfection before being led into a giant, deserted white hall where they were forced to wait, naked, for hours. It turned out, now she heard it all clearly, that the SS officers didn't know they were the passengers of a rescue train, and that as far as they were concerned, all trains were bound for Auschwitz, and that perhaps they were going to send them off with a stream of gas right then and there.

Seventy years have since gone by, and one can more or less piece together what happened there. Elsa Bloom-Weiss standing naked, alone in the women's line, no children of her own beside her. Eric huddled with the other men. Clara and her mother are nowhere in sight—they had entered a different car in Budapest.

I don't know what thoughts crossed her mind. Does that even need to be said? Even when it seems I'm disappearing, remember I'm in the picture. I believe I knew the girl Elsa Bloom had been, she could have been me, but now I am about to lose her entirely. I know Elsa Weiss is destined to one day arrive in Palestine and never speak of what happened to her, and maybe for that reason I should stop here. What business do I have with that thing she struggled to erase from her consciousness so she could carry on? Even if somewhere the so-called "simple version" exists, once she chose not to divulge it, the story belongs to no one and simplicity is far from it. A vast gulf stretches between us, I cannot skip over it, and I must remember that in the end life triumphed, life always triumphs over the great catastrophes, and even if we don't always see it that way, and sometimes sink into melancholic pessimism, life is ultimately in greater supply than death. And yet something compels me to continue. Memorial days and films, literature and academia and five decades of existence have allegedly taught me how to write, with a steady pen, about ashes and mud and a cold I have never known, without trembling. I have also learned how to phrase insoluble contradictions between the ability of the consciousness to say whatever it feels like, and the restrictions the conscience imposes on speech. In the past, I had found a form of compromise. I did not enter any camps, I did not invade any bodies, did not cross any borders, I did not dare. Others probably had to cross the border for me, while I settled for presenting fundamental questions about the limits of representation. Until I was suddenly afraid that my time was running out, and I knew that I actually wasn't certain of anything, not of the reality of the places I had visited, not of the sights revealed before me, not even of my own experiences. I had been only half present in all of them. I wish to revisit each one of them as if for the first time.

Elsa cast her gaze upon the long line snaking behind her. She could not see anyone she knew. The women and children circled around her naked like a tight ring, and she stood as if nailed in place. Standing for so long exhausted her. She shifted her body weight from side to side and wished she could get on her knees, but knew she mustn't draw attention to herself, and that in any case, she must be vigilant. She heard the buzzing of an electric razor coming from the direction of the showers and noticed a woman sitting there with the razor and clumps of hair piling up, and she started to itch, although she knew it was impossible, she did not have lice. The line of women before her was dwindling, and she felt the blood draining from her body and a terrible weakness assailing her, and she knew that they could do whatever they wished to her, that she could perform only the most basic, fragmented motions required of her, take a few steps, hold her hands open, spread her thighs, lower her head, that was more or less it, she knew, while the Ukrainian guards dragged her to the SS physician, whose hands wandered across her body and penetrated her private parts to smear them with Lysol. Her head was heavy and void of thoughts, she didn't even wonder about the events taking place internally. The shower mercilessly whipped her sheared scalp. The stinging disinfectant let loose a long moan from her mouth. At a certain point, but this was already after she had exited the showers, the guards realized a mistake had been made and stopped shaving heads. She was surprised to find the bundles of disinfected clothes waiting for them at the entrance of the hall, but the immaculate order only exacerbated her unease, and it seemed that it also unnerved the others, as they made their way back to their train in withdrawn silence.

She was more or less the last woman to have been shaved. And because the process came to a halt like a sudden epidemic, attacking only part of the camp and leaving the rest unscathed, the capriciousness of the entire event had become palpable. She was not indifferent. She realized that unbearable things were happening. She did not bear them. She moved slightly aside so as not to give into them. It was a form of saying goodbye, an utterly private cleansing ritual she carried out within herself, a wall she had erected between her past and her future. No matter how many strange hands invaded this ceremony, it was her ceremony and she performed it with pride. She did not even feel ashamed. Nor did her exposed body make her feel shame. The shame that had overwhelmed her as a child in the presence of her parents or teachers was more primal, set against the desired ideals she had failed to meet. What she felt now was something akin to awkwardness, as if she had been abducted to a foreign land and was seeking a way back, but there was no one to retrieve her, nothing and no one to return to. Eric's terror-stricken gaze attested to his understanding that he could no longer protect her. He hugged her and cried. She held back her tears. Her thick hair, which had hung loose down her back from a young age, sometimes coiled on her head like a crown, braided or gracefully tousled, had been ripped from her scalp. She could only wait and see what would grow back in its place. It was so awful, but it helped her not recognize herself. She was someone else. Even if she returned to Kolozsvár that moment, nothing would be the same. A woman in a coif, who stood next to her in the car, handed her a silk headscarf.

The change of plans gave rise to a swell of speculation and predictions. They received an update on recent developments. The Allied forces had advanced and liberated Strasbourg. British and Canadian troops had reached the city of Cannes. Kastner sent a reassuring telegram to the local leadership: There is no need to panic, there will be a short delay until another way is found to honor the deal and reach Portugal or Spain. On Saturday morning they approached Göttingen, and in the afternoon they turned toward Nuremberg. On their last night on the train, they stayed at Würzburg. At around nine o'clock Sunday morning, July 9th, they entered the Bergen-Belsen camp.

21

It was an odd prison, in which children and adults of all ages crammed into three-story bunks, the innocence of its inmates its widest common denominator, a prison that was run and supervised by criminals, an upside-down world that could have been experienced as a crazy game had it not become an absurd and taxing reality. Not because they had to do anything, but precisely because they had to do nothing, had to shrink their existence to nothingness, to diminish their existence into a battle over the perseverance of existence, a battle sustained by the memory of the promise that all this was temporary, that they would be released at some point. Confronted with the merciless possibility that had barreled down on them like a monster since they embarked on their journey that they would never have more time, that time might come to a complete and utter end, this sudden excess of time was a curious surprise. And yet, for those among them who had lost hope, time had lost its meaning. It froze as though deprived of its inherent continuity and rid itself of any expectations. It could not be used. It no longer served as a steady anchor that allows one to deviate from it back and forth in order to understand what is happening by way of comparison or imagination.

Before the car doors were opened and they disembarked from the train at what was revealed to be their final destination, she had not been able to take an interest in the names of the stations they had passed, not until the rumor of the assumed name sent the passengers into a frenzied panic. But now she wanted to know, as if by knowing the name she could decipher something about their destiny. They walked for a very long time. Some of the heavy equipment was loaded onto the truck that carried the elderly, the sick, and the children, but there seemed to be a shortage of trucks. She heard people bitterly complaining that the leaders were exploiting them, the same leadership that had assembled already at the beginning of the journey, by the Austrian border, according to the relative size of the Zionist parties and representatives of other groups, in an attempt to create a semblance of control amid the chaos. She had lost track of time and couldn't gauge how many kilometers they had traveled with their exhausted bodies, shriveled from the journey and the crippling hunger. She did her best to endure, lowering her gaze under the silk headscarf. Her baldness made her feel lighter and more exposed to the wind, and she was suddenly gripped by the childish desire for a caressing hand on her head, which she immediately fended off out of fear that she couldn't bear even her own touch. She struggled to aim her gaze higher, off the ground and away from the legs that marched on it, wearing a frozen expression that maintained the automatic motion and pace, which now seemed like the pace of existence, the temporary existence, she reminded herself, the sequence of actions that must be performed. She allowed herself to trail like a young girl after the others, and every time she saw and did not see the same things, dust, clothes, pieces of barbed wire strewn about; and when she looked up for a moment and stole a glance at the others, she encountered the same terror-stricken expressions of those who did not know where they were heading. She struggled to go with the lost, helpless flow, in the strange landscape, in a numb body. She knew they wouldn't walk for hours, it had to end eventually, and it wouldn't be as bad as it had been on the train, they were still outside, moving, what more could happen? A few people were presiding over the march, it seemed as though they knew more, she didn't doubt that, they had authority, even if it was their first time there and they appeared to be just as surprised as everyone else, they had connections, their status was evident in the way they spoke and the manner in which the others addressed them. She cast her gaze upon several children walking nearby and registered a few mischievous faces spared the tension, expressions that turned grim only when the children asked repeatedly: "Mom, what's going to happen?," the question answered with an effort not to betray a shred of despair, dismissed with a simple sentence they could cling to: "There are children your age here you can play with," "We're only going to be here a short while." It is good the children asked, you could think about it rationally instead of falling into the abyss.

They were put in the *Ungarnlager*, right beside the horror, in a separate compound designated for the Jews of "the Hungarian deal." They were supposed to be released soon, and weren't meant to see the bottom of the hierarchy of Bergen-Belsen's elaborate system, those who were subjected to the rules of a "normal" concentration camp; but when passing by the electric barbed-wire fences on the way to the open pits that served as latrines, a perforated strip located a great distance from the barracks, the watchtower's projector accompanying them in the dark like a pillar of cloud, they stumbled here and there upon the death-stricken ghosts dragging corpses crushed by forced labor, abhorrent sanitary conditions, and malnutrition. They saw, they had no way of not seeing, they found themselves witnessing a fate they had apparently evaded, a hell they would most likely be spared, and they could not do a thing, not help, not rally, not ask questions, not console, they were utterly paralyzed by what was taking place right in front them, and forced to be grateful that it was not their own lot.

However, those who had yet to enter the inferno but knew-and-didn't-know of its existence, might have fallen into the clutches of despair, even if they were still clad in civilian clothing, without the yellow badge, and carried a piece of paper and pencil and a book or phylacteries, even if they weren't subjected to forced labor but rather to the discipline of shifts, hauling jugs of water and food, cleaning, and performing roll calls that spanned half a day. Even if at least some of them were fortunate enough to remain with their families. Nothing had prepared them for this. They had been cut off from the world and resided in wet barracks under leaking roofs, their living area confined to the space between one bunk and the next, attempting in vain to control the movement inside it, to maneuver between clumps of earth and stones lest the entire barrack fill with mud whenever someone accidentally or maliciously started a violent commotion. They eyed each other with suspicion, with their heads hanging low, as if in denial of the extreme proximity that forced them to be exposed and to see and to listen to each other, to act as though it was an ordinary and self-evident routine, adamantly insisting on forgetting what they saw, on covering themselves with a veil of indifference, so that if they ever met in the future, they could start from the beginning as if none of this had ever happened.

The labor of life had become complicated precisely because of its fundamental simplicity—how to fill one's stomach, how best to divide, how to slice accurately, how to save crumbs. Those whose spendthrift or jovial nature was unaccustomed to restraint became irritable and bitter. The loaves of bread they were allotted resembled bricks in both shape and weight, 330 grams per person, better than what the rest of the camp was given; they were to be kept alive and provided just enough so they wouldn't die of starvation. Elsa was able to tear the loaf—without devouring it—into equal pieces that would last her a week. The restrained adult who had taken the gluttonous little girl's place mastered the practice of autosuggestion. She felt hunger without appetite, a hunger that could be satiated by a piece of bread. Since she tasted it in her imagination, she could command herself to pause, to hold back, to not even crave it, to repeat the cycle again and again, to dwell on it in order to rid herself of it. And yet, she was becoming hungrier by the day, the slices of sawdust turning into a coveted delicacy. She drank coffee in the mornings and at dinner, flavorless gray-black water that at times was tepid enough to warm her hands. The soup was brought daily in containers from the camp kitchen, accompanied by bland root vegetables, some of which she had never seen before and were probably used for feeding animals, cats or pigs, but there was no choice but to eat what she was given, to hold her nose to get over the sour smell of the beets and the urine and the rot and not notice what she was shoveling into her mouth, to swallow in moderation, just to get something into her stomach, just to make herself stronger. Sometimes, when someone must have been in an especially good mood, they were treated to potatoes, beef stew, blood sausages, crumbs of meat, even bean cholent. At first her throat refused the unpalatable mush and expelled it; then it gradually gave in. She would place a tiny morsel in her mouth and chew at length; afterward, if she did not vomit, she had to lie in bed, draw her knees to her stomach and curl into a fetal position until she calmed down; still, she stood in the food line the following day like everyone else, observing that just like the others she too would stare at the person doling food onto her mess tin, and secretly keep score with him—why did he give some people more than he gave her, taking offense at the solid substance burrowing at the bottom of the soup pot and preventing her from receiving the ration she deserved? (The surname Eric had bequeathed her had driven her to the bottom of the alphabet, which seemingly worked in her favor, but sometimes the name list was reversed, and she wished she could go back to being Bloom). Sometimes, when all she wanted was to be elsewhere, she sent Clara to take her place in the line, and remembered how she used to stand around in the kitchen, serving as her mother's apprentice, in order to lick the pots and the bottom of the cake bowl after the batter was poured into the baking pan and placed in the oven, how she used to dive deep into the dish and let her finger climb from the base and bring the thick liquid into her mouth, over and over, until the bowl shone in its cleanliness. "It can't be any cleaner than that," her mother would say facetiously, astonished by her daughter's ravenous appetite. Over time, the indulging element of their relationship disappeared, and she herself began listlessly cooking the recipes passed onto her by Grandma Rosa; for some reason, the only image of her she savored was her head bent over and sweating into the pot of matzo ball soup on Passover eve, imbuing the broth with a revolting yet curiously human saltiness. Now, when she aimed her finger at the indented bottom of her mess tin, it lacked any whimsy. It was the gesture of a homeless person.

22

People around her needed her help. You never let us help you, she was scolded with gratitude. She smiled awkwardly, learned to accept their assistance, took simple comforts in the children, thanked her good fortune for Clara and Mrs. Adler's presence in the Kolozsvár barrack, which was a kind of room they shared, she on the top wooden bunk and they on the two below her. This sleeping arrangement made sense, and despite the crude presence of the hay mattress and the gray military blanket, the familiar faces made it somehow friendly. To her surprise, she found in her suitcase handwritten notes her mother had hidden between the folds of her socks like tiny treasures, greetings wishing her safe travels. When had she had the time?

At first, they failed to notice Mrs. Adler's decline. But gradually it manifested in her voice, her eyes, in her lack of interest in their conversations; then one day she stopped doing her hair and makeup. That day she woke up for the morning roll call and sat slouched in the bunk in her robe, declaring a strike, a strike against herself. She paid no attention to the makeup purse placed beside her, the small mirror with which she communed each morning remaining in her bag like an abandoned object. Clara pleaded with her to powder her face and make herself presentable, to look around her. "We're better off than most, it could be worse." But Mrs. Adler wouldn't listen. "This is absurd," she said angrily, "I don't know what I was thinking." And Elsa saw an entirely different woman before her, no longer the Mrs. Adler she had known since childhood; she never imagined how foreign a familiar face could become, and wondered whether it had indeed happened all of a sudden, or whether she did not want to see what had been happening to Mrs. Adler because it might have taught her something about herself, about what was taking place inside her. She felt a twinge in her heart thinking about Mother, that perhaps she could have treated her differently, not judged her so harshly, now telling herself the obvious, that her mother did the best she could, and at any rate, she had good intentions, and perhaps the task of raising children was more than she could handle; and after all, when Elsa herself failed to conceive, even though she agonized over it for a while, it was convenient for her to believe that nature was refusing to bequeath her with gifts of which she was unworthy, gifts she could not adamantly attest to truly wanting or needing. But those last few years could also have been lived better, she could have laughed more, had she not been in such a hurry to pull away, or had she stayed another year in Paris; had she not rushed to marry so young. When she couldn't fall asleep she would look at the women around her, at the odd intimacy that had developed among them.

They wouldn't let Mrs. Adler stay in bed: "At least get up, Mom," Clara implored; they let her stand beside her bunk during roll call on the condition that she put herself together. Clara combed her hair. "You mustn't let them win." "What do they care if I sleep or stand, what does it matter," her mother replied. "That's exactly it, everything matters, there has to be order." But it was beyond her grasp, the absolute order required within the absolute disorder, the order that was apparently the only way their executioners could survive what they were doing, to enforce the law in hell. Mrs. Adler felt that chaos was chaos, she was unwilling to pretend there was some kind of order here that she could respect. Elsa actually liked this, the little war Mrs. Adler was waging, which brought out the best in her, the ridicule of the aristocratic matron whose world—a world of wheeling and dealing, misdemeanors and sidesteps—had been taken from her and yet she remained doggedly loyal to it in her complaints about boredom and the women around her, as if believing that soon the fog would lift and she would grab the banister and link her free arm in her husband's, who had suffered a heart attack and passed away sometime during the first year of the war, and together they would stroll back to their apartment at the end of yet another evening in which she had drunk herself into a stupor. He would slip off her shoes, lay her heavy body on the bed, and she would sink into a deep and disturbed sleep from which, as after every evening of inebriation, she would wake the next morning unable to remember a thing. "Are you sure I said that? Impossible. It's strange how a person can be simultaneously able to be and not to be." "In your case, that is *not* the question," Mr. Adler would say, thus concluding the initiation ceremony into the sobriety of daylight. "But Mom, you can't, you're absolutely right but you can't," Clara insisted, because the young, burly woman with the steel eyes would soon approach in her high boots and white-fur gloves, and reprimand her with the same fervor she would use to strike three-year-olds across their faces if they failed to stand when she entered the barrack, or tear the prayer book of the old woman who didn't stretch the blanket across her bunk in military fashion. "You really don't want to get on her bad side," Clara said. "What do I care, I'll give her a piece of my mind." Quite often such an exchange, merely by arguing her point, was enough to appease her. And yet, she gradually weakened. She could not bear the animal feed in the form of beets, and they had to talk to her like a child: Look how your neighbor is eating and how that aunt is relishing this delicacy; and they would spoon feed her, or tell her it was actually a different dish, one that went by several names, and then name one of her favorite dishes. They wouldn't relent, and even applied pressure to make her brush her teeth. "We're taking you for a shower," once every two weeks, which she especially hated, the slippery wooden floorboards, the miserable, bruised bodies she had to witness—gaunt and blue, the sight of the concave stomachs of formerly full-figured women who had once carried their voluptuous curves with pride.

They helped her reach the toilet in the single small cubicle at the end of the barrack, a door separating it from the rest of the large hall; ushered her into the line of women standing there impatiently day and night; saved or traded pieces of toilet paper or rags for her. "Elsa," she said to her one evening with the twinkle of someone about to share a secret, "I always knew you were a tenderhearted child." She said this right before they had to finish dinner and prepare for bed. "I'm not tired at all," she would announce at this hour, like a child complaining about lights-out at summer camp. The darkness they were sentenced to every night at ten brought her back to reality. When she fell into hysterical fits, in which she mumbled meaningless sentences that grew shorter and shorter and tightened around her neck, the two stood on either side of her, hovering over her back and leaning their entire weight against it to alleviate the tension that had built up in her body, until she stopped trembling.

23

In my dreams, Weiss was closer to me than ever. In the first dream she taught the children of Bergen-Belsen French and English. She entered with a bright smile, closed the door behind her to keep out the belligerent wind, and greeted them. There were six of them, and she divided her attention equally, as if tearing a challah at the Shabbat table. They were utterly devoted to her, seeking her presence even after class. She let them cling to her, brushed a hand through their hair, examined their fingernails, asked if there were holes in their socks, if the soles of their shoes were still intact—they knew she was willing to trade her own bread to help them and their parents find solutions. She picked up a shoe for demonstration, lifting it high and breaking into song: "One kilometer on foot wears out the sole," and the children joined in, forming a choir under her conductorship and gradually diverging into polyphony, *"un ki ki ki un ki lo lo, un kilometre."* She seemed so resourceful, as if seeking ways to sidestep reality, to relish her teaching, to invent a *"mnémotechnique,"* as she stressed before them, to maintain a clear and coherent presence so they would continue to believe the world was a place worthy of living in, that one day it would be possible to return to it, that one day, they surely would.

She harnessed all the knowledge in her possession, and most likely the knowledge she had never imagined she possessed, in order to create a world for them predicated on the words they learned to say together. "The tongue can speak words that bring life or death," she told them. "You believe that?" one of the children asked her. "Yes, certainly. For instance, when war or peace is declared, when vows are taken, or when promises are made to bring people from one end of the world to another. In each of these examples, you can say that words sustain or destroy." "And when you're just chatting?" She laughed in response, started to act out metaphors, spreading her arms, and gathered them under her wings in Hungarian, English, and French. I recognized the Hungarian, even though I cannot recognize it when I'm awake. In the dream I knew that while awake I heard nothing but her silence.

She taught language in its deepest sense, making accessible things that weren't within reach. One of the children asked if she was referring to the story they learned in Torah class about the descendants of Shem who told each other: "Let us build us a city and a tower, whose top may reach unto heaven; and let us make us a name," because they merely said it and the city was built. The bespectacled girl said that because they wanted to ordain a single language in the Tower of Babel, God had been punishing us all ever since. "You think all this is God's punishment?" "My parents say it's punishment for a Godless world."

She encouraged them to memorize with her the fundamental forms of language, the rules, the genders, the verb conjugations. They were everywhere but Bergen-Belsen. Any ounce of information etched in her memory from the grand edition of *Encyclopedia*

Britannica, whose twenty-nine volumes proudly shared space on three separate shelves in her parents' guest room, served her to compile a glossary, which allowed the children to stroll through produce stands in markets, to plan elaborate feasts, sail and fish, go picnicking outdoors, to compose and solve crossword puzzles about sweets. On a full stomach they practiced dry swimming, standing before her in a horizontal line and mimicking the front crawl, the butterfly and breast stroke she had demonstrated. They galloped like knights, sang humorous songs around the campfire, got down on their knees and followed seven-year-old Hannah, who had been spending most of her time since arriving at the camp on all fours, glancing at them behind a stool, and replied to her angry barking with a mélange of animal languages, every animal they could think of, mammals and predators, like in Noah's Ark, as if they were indeed the species God had chosen to protect from extinction, and would be set free once the flood receded.

24

At first glance, one could fail to notice the beauty of Clara's face; the pensive blue eyes, the soft features framed by full lips painted a dark red, that along with her pinched, freckled nose, created the impression of an alluring sensuality and mischievous innocence. The lively and bold expression, punctuated with short, straight black hair that she had cut herself since high school, was now fortified by a wide body, which thickened over time and made her seemingly invulnerable. "Clara is always asking about you," Mother would say in a tone alternating between reprimand and enticement whenever they returned from a visit to the Adlers, to see whether she could reignite her daughter's feelings for her old friend, to whom she had stopped talking around the age of fourteen. In return, Elsa would inquire after Clara's well-being and with that end the conversation. She no longer joined the joint family trips. She retreated into her own world and Clara into hers, graduating high school and proceeding to study painting at the arts academy, and rarely did their paths cross—barring that awkward conversation when they bumped into each other on the street upon Elsa's return from Paris, a conversation that arose most likely because Elsa felt an instant intimacy toward her, the kind that can only be felt, rightfully or not, toward a childhood friend, and which was accompanied by the urgent need to unburden herself to someone and share the heartache she carried inside her over the American with whom she had fallen in love the very first moment she heard his voice one morning, when he was speaking to the chambermaid in the corridor of the boardinghouse, a voice sweeter than any she had ever heard before, which beckoned her to seek its owner, Christopher Roseo, a literature student who was writing a thesis on Stendhal, and with whom she spent nearly every waking hour until his return to Berlin. He sang opera arias from heart, she told Clara with twinkling eyes, and he teased her about her impending wedding, but it was over and done with months ago, she had lost contact with him, there was no point in continuing it, they would have never made it anyway, and actually, she stressed, nothing really happened between them, a platonic love she had let perish. Clara mumbled something about the everlasting flame of stolen loves and then said, "Why the hell are you doing it, Elsa?" and she replied something along the lines of, "Because Mother expects me to," and Clara said, "Then you're stupid." Elsa couldn't remember what thoughts had crossed her mind that moment, she was probably embarrassed, because she knew Clara was right, that it was a type of stupidity, and at any rate certainly not a good enough reason to do anything, but who better than Clara knew the driving influence their mothers had on their lives, she had no right to judge her, and yet still felt that Clara was truly surprised, even disappointed by her, as if she expected something else of her and didn't think her capable of being so cowardly and characterless. "You're stupid." Not stupid at school or in her accomplishments, but afflicted by a different kind of stupidity, one that pertained to her ability to understand herself, to define her boundaries first and foremost to herself, and consequently to others, what was good and what was bad for her. And several weeks later Clara attended the wedding, and Elsa felt as though Clara's expression read somewhere between an apology and regret at having been perhaps too cruel or decisive, and who was she to intervene in her affairs anyway, but they never spoke of it, and who knows, maybe by now Clara had forgotten all about it, whereas only Elsa remained with that tired, morose, and bitter taste of defeat she had suffered at her own hand.

Three weeks later, Clara began to feel ill. Her bowels, which had always been weak and prone to irritability, couldn't endure the change; her temperature spiked, accompanied by unrelenting stomach pains and headaches that exhausted her. Elsa made sure she would not have to go outside for morning roll calls and instead could be counted, like her mother, inside the barrack. Clara refused to lie in the infirmary, and waited for Elsa to be done with roll call and the lessons she taught, about two hours each day, after consenting to the request of the internal leadership to teach beginner's English and French, so they could talk, they had to talk about the past, which elucidated at least what they had been, the lives they had lived, as well as what they had failed at, and what had not yet come to pass and existed only in the realm of expectation. Now she and Clara had become dependent on each other again, recreating against the background of wooden barracks and windowless stone buildings the ability they had shared as children to stage extreme scenes, although this time they did not have the luxury to stop playing when they became tired. They remembered how they loved to shut away in their rooms while their mothers chatted in the kitchen, how they stuck their fingers in their underwear and then licked them ecstatically. They recalled how they tried to lie on top of each other and coordinate their body movements, Elsa's mouth clumsily fumbling toward Clara's, but their heads bumped and their shoulders collided. "We were in complete disharmony." "Yes, and we did our best to keep from bursting into laughter." Little Elsa once hid her shoes in someone's backyard so she could come home and say they had disappeared. "Did they vanish into thin air?" her mother asked her. "I lost them," she lied through her teeth. And eventually she received new shoes. But even as a teenager, when she strayed from the magical logic of the lost and found, the lost and fabricated, and was faced with irrecoverable loss, it carried the promise of growth. The loss helped her mature, or at least that's what she had believed. Now, as they both stood before a loss for which there was no compensation, they remembered every last detail of the games, books, people, lullabies, as if reverting back into the nothingness from which it seemed everything might begin anew.

They also spoke about her and Eric. She knew they were going to get divorced. He was in a good mood. He slept in the youth movement barrack and could have snuck into her bunk at night as the other couples did, but they had stopped sleeping together long ago, and there was no point in pretending.

The days preceding Clara's death were almost completely erased from Elsa's memory. Clara's condition had deteriorated and she could no longer stay in the barrack. She was admitted to the infirmary and placed on a middle bunk, below a young girl ill with dysentery and above a young man who lay unconscious with typhus. The doctor's mother, Mrs. Shtark, who tended to the patients, concocted a sauerkraut brine to ease her pain. Elsa tried spoon-feeding her. "It reminds me of the chocolate milk you once made me," Clara said, and with tears added that she knew she wasn't going to make it. On the morning of August 8th, Elsa warmed her hands against her cup of coffee, murky and grainy as always, and hummed to herself a tune she liked, until the melodic line was abruptly interrupted by Mrs. Adler's scream.

Elsa stayed in the camp for ten more days. On August 18th, five weeks after they first arrived at the camp, she learned she was being released. She was finishing up a class and one of the leaders, she couldn't remember who, came and told her she was on the short list of those being released now; the others would be released later on, they didn't know yet when, and she must get ready at once and gather her belongings because they had to reach the train by foot. Others provided more details: she was among the three hundred eighteen people being transferred to a refugee camp in Switzerland, at Caux, Zionists and religious Jews and seculars like her, who had no distinct affiliation. Most of the group was comprised of children and the elderly. There was no time for explanations—how the list was compiled or if there was any logic to it. One way or another, she was unworthy in every respect, and although she knew something about the surprisingly powerful forces that erupted from within her at that time, just like the anxiety she had developed in the seemingly steady and affluent world she came from, she didn't think this prize was awarded to her for exemplary behavior. She felt as though an anonymous force, something as arbitrary as the toss of a coin, a creature that probably wasn't even human, was sparing her. She ran to the youth movement barracks to talk to Eric, cried and told him she wanted to stay. "Are you mad? Don't you dare even consider it. The rest of us will follow later, it's a matter of a few weeks." "How can you say that with such confidence?

Up until now everything has gone wrong." "You can't say no. It would be insanity." She knew he was right. "But it'll be winter soon," she said worriedly. "I expect we'll come much sooner. Take what you're offered, think of yourself, think of the advice you'd give someone else, the only advice worth giving, never turn down what you're given." She soberly knew that her good fortune was her bad fortune, a miracle that tightened around her neck like a noose. She should have been stronger, not let him persuade her. Some weakness had come over her, a weakness she never compensated for. Someone wanted her to be saved, or perhaps to suffer even more; she knew with complete clarity that the survivor is doomed to suffer. She returned to her barrack. Mrs. Adler was sprawled across her bunk. Elsa rushed to her and sobbed bitterly, refusing to calm down. They sat in a long embrace. "Get up and go, my child," Mrs. Adler told her softly. "We'll meet again." Elsa collected her few belongings and joined the convoy awaiting her outside. No one said a word to her. She considered whether to say goodbye to her pupils, but her nerves failed her, and she left without looking back. Some stood and watched her walk away until she became a tiny dot and disappeared.

Their convoy marched for hours until they reached the civilized passenger train that awaited them. They were on their way to The World of Yesterday. Those left behind at the camp ended up forced to wait many more months, until December 2nd, before they joined the others in Switzerland. By then their living conditions had worsened. Three more people died. From August 18th to December 2nd, six babies were born. Seventeen prisoners were transferred to other blocks in the camp and were never released.

Now Elsa Weiss was the privileged among the privileged.

25

She found herself in a sanatorium of the kind Grandma Rosa used to patronize after becoming a widow, the kind of place that depressed her mother because of the Jewish women who went to such health resorts to take in the air after the death of their husbands, spending days on end playing card games, choosing routes for short walks in order to feel they were in motion, and eating pastries—her mother's greatest fear was "becoming like them," or "ending up like them." The spacious hotel rooms had been converted into a displaced-persons camp, but since the passengers weren't many, she received a room of her own in which she could finally be alone. Few people strolled outside, many chose to hole up in their rooms like her. There was little traffic on the roads during the day, mostly private cars that cleared the way for trucks loaded with more refugees. For the first few days she preferred bolting the window of her room and withdrawing into her silence, even though the silence weighed heavily on her and she feared she would lose track of time completely. The bell of the white Lutheran church, commanding the distant mountainside with noble, reserved elegance, gave the signal for daybreak. She opened her eyes to the rivers of light that penetrated the dark green curtain, but remained in bed for a long period without being able to coax her body up, her eyes wandering across the white ceiling to come to rest on a tiny speck on the wall lamp. The pristine sheets pulled tight across the bed, the soft, fluffy blanket that lay on her body like a healing poultice, the water that poured from the taps in abundance, the clean towels that hung across the bath railing in impeccable symmetry, all invited her to relax her muscles. The clear mountain air that refreshed the bed sheets gradually expelled that smell from her nose. It was all real, she told herself. They were straight facts, she knew those facts, she did not even have to commit them to memory, and that somehow reassured her, to know exactly what happened, what they call historical truth, plain and simple, a truth you could either surrender to or rise up against, but not alter. How long had it been since she was home, she had no home, would she ever have a home? She had an existence; of that she was certain. She had a body that enabled her to move. She was subjected to conflicting powers, but never really bothered to examine what she was feeling. She didn't need to touch herself to discover that it was her, that she, Elsa Weiss, the daughter of Shmuel and Leah Bloom, was alive. But who was that person who was still alive? What was still alive inside her?

At night she moaned and groaned, now that she could let go, without a single soul around; she woke with a start, her throat full of phlegm, aching from shouting, and sank back into a troubled sleep from which she woke late, heavy and ragged from dreams. She stepped outside briefly, and overcome with exhaustion rushed back to her room to sleep. Twice a week a chambermaid appeared with a mop and rags, swiftly dusting the table and cabinets, wiping the window, vacuuming the carpet, scrubbing the bathroom, and changing her sheets in utter silence, with a solicitous look tinged with both terror and compassion. The impersonal service, its tenacious and neat rhythm, prompted her to recover, as someone subjected to a hidden struggle between destruction and rehabilitation; but rather than having a moderating effect, this struggle widened the gap between her and the world. There was something both difficult and insipid in the splendor around her. The harmonious straight lines, the water gurgling in every direction, the jingle of bells on the sturdy cows, were all procured effortlessly, as if apathetic. She didn't need them. She refused to admire her surroundings with the ungratefulness of a refugee rebuffing the abundance that exists for its own sake, an untimely abundance whose sheer fullness defied her. She refused to take in the normal landscape, to rush at the spread on the dining room table—eggs, turnips, margarine, rye bread, and end-of-summer fruits, riches she had long ago put behind her. She felt neither hunger nor thirst, and drank and ate as if forced. Waiters fussed over her, offering coffee and tea as if she was a regular guest, as if she was a returning guest to the sanatorium, and now she was required to truly recover from something, but she knew she would never be able to recover from this. She would not let herself readjust to things of beauty, to the luxurious town wrapped like a box of chocolates, a clouded paradise lying wide open, neither trampled on nor disfigured by their presence. At times it seemed this prim and processed nature was overpowering and defeating them. They were the survivors of a collapsed civilization and it hosted them, not with a warm welcome, but cautiously, suspiciously, as still as a postcard. Stiff representatives of welfare and relief agencies—who projected discontent over the fact that their guests were not the usual bourgeois but rather the desolate

Europeans, terrifying figures they had to serve for nothing in return—waited to reequip them for life, to allow them to put on new strength as if changing costumes in a backstage dressing room, before returning to the front stage of history. She saw the recoiling and frightened faces of the locals who were robbed of their blessed equanimity, and the awestruck faces of the refugees as they witnessed the dogged persistence of world order, even if now it seemed more absurd than ever, as they reflected on what had once upon a time been a comforting respite among the mountains and limpid, undisturbed lakes, and was now a life in limbo, suspended and facing the unknown.

How could they think they would somehow get away with it, that the events would pass them by, that they would be saved, how did they dare believe they were protected, how did they refuse all that time to even consider leaving? In reality they never felt any urgency, she knew that was the plain truth, their desperate clinging to the place that was their home, a fierce, conclusive emotion that had nothing to do with beauty, not even with comfort, but with that certainty they each held, apparently, that that was the land on which they could continue to grow, whose language and landscapes they loved with the innocence of young love. Now she already allowed herself to feel abandoned, subjected to the daunting fear that she might forget them, that with each passing day, if she did not make the effort to conjure up their images, she would lose something of their voices, their gazes, that something prosaic might push them aside to a place that was only in her reach when it charged at her in her dreams. She envisioned her childhood room, which remained intact after she left home, the guest room in her and Eric's apartment, the study in which she slept below shelves packed with books; she peered at clear images, specific moments etched more sharply than thousands of others, what she allowed herself to see as a girl, what she merely glanced at, what she had ignored, and all those sights she never fully took in with her eyes but stored in her body, and which spawned her sadness.

In the bag she rushed to pack before they moved to the ghetto she had placed letters, notes, and two journals she saved from trips with her parents from the two consecutive summers after Jan's departure, when, to ease the pain of his absence, they traveled together to the Low Countries and to Rome. She opened one of the journals and remembered awkwardly how she had written down elaborate descriptions of the view and reported on churches and museums, but without writing a single word about herself, a single word about them, a single word about their interaction, as if she were seeking to please someone, but who? With no one destined to read these journals, they remained a testimony without a witness, the pages leaving no trace of their author. She felt she was connected to her parents in some inconspicuous way, beyond their family ties, which at times she never even felt and at other times wished to escape—that she was realizing their fate through her body, that their destiny had yet to be determined. She knew they had been sent to their deaths, and it troubled her that she didn't sense it the day they were deported, or perhaps she did, she was certain she did, but never really believed it, half-expecting to find them wherever she went, scanning her new surroundings, perhaps they were there, maybe despite everything they had still found a way to settle in a new country.

Her lips remained sealed. To the extent she could, she avoided the company of others, reducing it to a bare minimum, left her room and entered the hallway cautiously, always choosing the stairs over the elevator, so as not to come into contact with the other passengers, who, while remaining physically close, had already grown distant; as if they already knew the relationship between them wouldn't last, that what made it so fateful also rendered it fragile, a relationship that had to be sidestepped and somehow denied. She greeted people with a brief nod and hurried off, avoiding questions. Perhaps it was then that she developed the skill of being seen and disappearing at the same time, of navigating her way along the streets, slim figured—her hair had grown back and she had removed the headscarf—without anyone being able to say whether she had crossed their path. What she fended off was precisely what she could not contain. Clara had told her in one of their conversations in the camp that that was the source of her sanity, that she must guard it, not let anyone in, otherwise she'd go mad. She knew Clara was right, but what did that sanity leave her with?

Representatives of the Jewish Agency started milling about outside, saying they had to wait patiently a few more months to obtain an immigration certificate to Israel. The war was not over yet, and since she wasn't a member of any youth movement, and had not undergone training, it might take her more time than the others. They tried to tell her that Israel was something entirely different, far from the afflictions of Europe, untouched by decay and destruction, in order to instill in her a pioneering spirit, but she remained indifferent and skeptical, she didn't believe there was a single place on the globe that wasn't afflicted. She considered remaining in Switzerland, descending the mountain slope to some other place in the French canton, even though she knew it was a futile possibility that would never grant her peace, and maybe it was best she returned, maybe she indeed ought to go home, she didn't even dare voice that idea, she didn't have the strength to fight Jan, who had started pressuring her into coming; in the letter she received from him several weeks after her arrival in Caux he informed her of his efforts to expedite her certificate and implored her to immigrate, inviting her to stay in his apartment in Tel Aviv, with his wife, Hannah, and his little boy, Yoel, until she found a suitable place. Twenty years had gone by since he left the family home in Kolozsvár. She knew about some of his trials and tribulations, about his years at Kibbutz Ma'agan, where he initially settled, about the stifling disappointment in the communal lifestyle, about his decision to move to the city and study engineering at the Hebrew University, where he met his love, Hannah, who had completed her training as a Torah teacher at the David Yellin Seminar. It was only when they resumed their communication in Switzerland that she learned of his marriage during the war and of the birth of their son in its final days. Twenty years had passed since they last saw each other, and when she sat down to write him she felt an odd mix of longing and unease, as if she couldn't truly remember him, as if she was actually considering— as if it was up to her at this stage—to choose one way or another. Had she seriously considered going elsewhere? Her longing for home was suppressed by her overwhelming sense of orphanhood. She vaguely knew she wouldn't return. While she had gradually become determined to go to Palestine, her determination was not nourished by hope. She feared she would always feel like an immigrant, that she would carry that curse, that Palestine would be a land of exile and not a haven of promise, and she asked herself whether she would ever be able to find a way in, persevere with something or someone, or perhaps find a replacement for the major things, for which she was never built, they intimidated her, she sensed danger in their meaning; and it was possible that once again, as always, she had no choice but to back off and let external forces carve out some kind of course she couldn't plan, that was out of her control. No one actually asked her if she wanted to immigrate. Why did she do it? To appease Jan? Because she was thinking of herself? Or not thinking of herself? There were moments during which she spoke to herself in second person, as if in disbelief—was that really how you felt? Was that what you knew? She asked herself whether something could happen in her life that would render it precious again.

In early December she waited with the other guests in the lobby of the Esplanade Hotel. A few days earlier, they had been informed that the remaining train passengers had been released and were making their way to Switzerland. The agency representatives would drive them from the train station to the hotel, in order to prevent crowding, they stressed, and she of course preferred not to accompany them but to wait in the corner of the spacious entrance hall, almost in hiding. Anxiously, she glanced at the horde of people slowly cramming into the lobby. Her body trembled, and in vain she ordered it to calm down. Among the hundreds of people streaming into the hall with tired steps, she spotted his face. He walked toward her, very thin, disheveled, his hair longer and faded, his skin taut and lashed by the wind and rain. "Elsa," he drew out her name, weighing every letter like a trader of precious stones in the presence of a diamond for the first time. "Elsa," he repeated, inhaling the two syllables of her name and staring at her, mesmerized. It seemed to her that she might have stalled before replying. "Eric." "I'm so happy," he said. She smiled. "Eric," she repeated his name. "So am I." If their shattered lives had retained any of their former simplicity, it was in the names they uttered to each other. He reached out his hand to take her arm and pulled her body into his. She placed her head on his shoulder and silently sobbed. With his other hand he brushed aside her boyish, unruly cowlick. They stood completely still, and then she shook him off in a panic, people were approaching them and she wanted them to find a quiet place to speak. "Maybe we could go up to your room?" But the reading room was empty and she led him there and when they sat down she asked him to tell her about himself. So much time had passed. "My parents . . . You already know," she told him. "How did you find out?" she asked. "Like everyone else." She gathered her breath and blurted out the words she had planned to say to him, and suddenly wasn't sure if she really meant them. "I had a lot of time to think." "That was never good for you," he replied. "You're right." She smiled. "I also thought about it a lot. I was hoping . . ." "I think there's no hope for us. You deserve a relationship . . ." He shrugged in dismissal. "I saw how easily you—" she insisted. "It's meaningless," he interrupted her, "you're all that matters." She flinched. She knew he really meant it, as if he had prepared himself to fight her. He had never fought her before. He leaned into her in search of her lips, which parted for him. "It's not sacrilegious to want it," he said. "That's not it." "I think that for you it is." He gathered her into his arms, pulled her up from the chair and paved their way to the corridor, told her to guide them to her room, entered, locked the door behind them and pressed her against him, propped her gaunt body against one of his knees, and starting ruffling her blouse. She removed his shirt and pinched the lean, sinewy flesh, as if rediscovering a body she had not remembered a thing about, tracing a finger across a scar that had formed a groove above his left eyebrow and lent a toughness to his boyish face, tried to fumble toward him cautiously, but her body was beyond her control and invited him inside her. They lay on the bed, floating on top of each other as if carrying the weightlessness of their youth again, light as a feather. He touched her lips with his finger and placed her small face in the palm of his hand. "You silly girl," he said. Then his expression turned somber. "You can't do it, Elsa." One day you'll thank me, she wanted to tell him but held back, it was arrogant, and she instantly felt overwhelmed with regret that her passion once again had overpowered her, fickle as it was, rendering her so vulnerable and so misleading; embarrassed, she turned to face the white wall and rubbed her back against his stomach for a long time, then retreated and curled up at the edge of the bed. When she turned back to face him again, he was already sitting up. She grew pale. "I'm so sorry, Eric," she said. He rose, got dressed, turned his back to her and closed the door behind him. She got up to open the window. It was already late in the day. Over the next two days she did not go down to the lobby. On the third day, at the breakfast table, she learned that the groups designated for training had been relocated to a different hotel in Montreux.

In Caux, she received the news that the war had ended. But what did that mean, the war had ended? Caux was not an occupied territory, and in the days following the announcement more and more refugee convoys rolled into the village. She experienced no sense of elation. She remained sprawled on the bed, tossing and turning, too many unreadable routes etched on her body. She assumed they would easily arrange a divorce that would free both her and Eric. She thought of other men she had met during all those months, but the thought evoked no appeal or eagerness, even when she heard that someone she had once been interested in had gotten married. For a few fleeting moments, she felt jealous.

But jealous of what? Not of the fact that someone else had taken her place, a place that was never meant for her. She didn't want what others allegedly had and was withheld from her. She didn't want a companion for this life, didn't want any further burdens. Perhaps she envied the ability of others to accept the assets civilized life offered them, a life from which she had exiled herself. She recognized this with complete clarity in the resort town, faced with the masses of refugees that flooded the mountains, knew that she too was a refugee in the active sense of the word, a self-exiled refugee, that she did not want to, or could not, and now did not have to keep up appearances or pretend; she wished for nothing at all. She realized that in fact she had stopped feeling, as if the lust she had known had left her, that she no longer desired to sink her teeth into a beloved dish, or a beloved person, or to hold onto a body or anything else out of devotion. She was free and entirely on her own. No one was waiting for her; she wasn't tethered to a single soul. She would not allow herself a family, another family.

26

But she had a family. And in those long months that passed from the time the war had ended and until her documents were arranged, months during which she remained in Caux and began giving private English lessons to the local children, Jan had not only taken care of the certificates, but also ensured she wouldn't have to stay in the detainee camp at Atlit upon her arrival in Palestine, as she had a family to host her and take care of her. "I hope I won't be a burden. I'll start looking for an apartment as quickly as possible," she wrote him in one of her brief letters. "It's not a problem, Elinka, you know that, we're happy to have you."

The extended period during which she stayed with Jan, Hannah, and Yoel before renting a one-room apartment nearby on Ben Yehuda Street was almost entirely erased from her memory. Her concerns grew heavier as she made the convoluted journey from Switzerland to the bottom of the Italian boot and finally to the ship, concerns that were accompanied by a troubling bewilderment about herself. She didn't understand what was happening to her, where everyone left inside her had gone; they couldn't have simply faded and disappeared; this untraversable distance pained her and hollowed out her heart. At the Atlit harbor she was approached by a silver-haired man with a tanned, pockmarked face, taller than Father and of a lighter complexion; he hugged her and kissed her and bawled, shook her body relentlessly, repeating over and over, "My little sister, I can't believe it," and then, "Hannah and Yoel are waiting at home." He took both her suitcases and led her to a scalding hot Ford Tudor. "You'll get used to it, thirty degrees in the shade, but there is no shade," he said, smiling as he rolled down the windows. "It'll take us about an hour and a half or two to get home." And then, as if to alleviate the silence that suddenly stretched between them, he pointed out places along the way, Mount Carmel and Zikhron Ya'akov and Binyamina and Netanya and Herzliya, offering a detailed description of the characteristics of each type of settlement and why they had decided, in spite of everything, he and Hannah, who was born in Jerusalem, to set up camp in Tel Aviv. "I think you'll like Tel Aviv," he said, injecting his voice with enthusiasm. "This is where it all happens," he said, now referring to the steadily increasing traffic. "There are cafes and theaters and concerts; of all the cities in Israel it's the most similar to Europe." He added: "And the beach, Elinka, you can swim. You like swimming, right?"

In anticipation of her arrival they had divided their enclosed balcony, which faced a small, quiet street near Ben Yehuda, erecting a screen to create a private area for her and furnishing it with a bed, desk, and dresser. Hannah gave her a warm welcome; "I've heard so much about you," she said, and took her on a tour of the apartment to show her where everything was so she could make herself at home; and when she noticed Elsa wiping the beads of sweat off her forehead, she explained that the humidity seeped through the walls, and suggested she keep the balcony window open during the night for the breeze to flow in, but to make sure to close the blinds from the early sunrise, which might wake her up. "You'll have to get used to it. The air is drier in Jerusalem, the humidity here is awful," Hannah said. Their eyes met for a moment and Elsa said, "Nice apartment," and Hannah felt uncomfortable with the compliment. "Small apartment," she rushed to reply, "but sufficient for our needs, until Yoel grows up," and immediately suggested they sit down for a small meal. "An Israeli dinner. This is what we eat here in the evening," she said apologetically, arranging a display of finely-chopped salad, white cheese, sliced bread, and hard-boiled eggs on the Formica kitchen table. "I'm taking Yoel to his nursery school in the morning and from there going to my school. You'll have time to settle in and get to know Tel Aviv a little. I understand we're in the same profession. You're a French teacher, right?" she tried again. "They might ask you to undergo further training," she cautiously suggested. "Elsa must be very tired, it's too soon to talk practicalities," Jan said. Hannah persisted: "Yoel was so looking forward to finally meeting his aunt from his father's side, say hello to Aunt Elsa, Yoeli," she said, her voice a pitch higher. That phrase, "Aunt Elsa," grated in her ear for some reason; she squinted, remaining glued to her chair and without picking up the toddler, who now braved a questioning stare. He was a skinny boy who apparently took after Hannah's side of the family more than theirs; he had inherited Jan's bright eyes and the smile that shone in his dimples, in stark contrast to the sorrow that poured from his gaze. She smiled at Hannah awkwardly. "I'm not good with babies," she said with a certain impatience. "Actually, I'm not so great with adults either." She folded her arms and pressed them against her waist. "It's an adjustment period," Hannah quickly offered. "After everything you've gone through . . ." she added, and looked at Jan with concern. "You have to think ahead," Jan said. "Jan always thought ahead," Elsa said to Hannah. "Even as a boy he was already thinking long-term." She wondered where those words had come from, and instantly fell silent. "It's his nature, always planning," Hannah went along with her. "Even when we met in Jerusalem, he was already talking about where we would live, what we would do and how much—" "Elsa is very tired, she doesn't want to hear anecdotes about our life," Jan interrupted her. "It's fine," Elsa said, rushing to her aid, "I'd love to hear about you two." They looked at Yoel, who was now sitting on the bare floor strewn with white paper, doodling with a pencil. "He's a quiet boy. He can keep himself busy for hours," Hannah said, "even though sometimes he gets bored. He needs a sibling." "I remember how long I waited for Elsa," Jan said. "When you came into the world I was almost ten; I was so happy." Elsa picked at the food on her plate, stabbing a piece of cucumber and chewing it slowly. "You're not hungry?" "The boat ride made me nauseous," she replied. "You're so thin, my sister." She remembered that when he left home she had weighed more, and started combing her hand through her hair, asking herself again what was wrong with her, if it was obvious she was angry about something, not that she knew what that something was, it wasn't as though he held it against her for having been *right all along*; he never said *I told you so*, not even in the letters he sent her in Switzerland, he never said anything even remotely along those lines, and at any rate that wasn't what she was angry about, his sobriety, the sobriety that never rubbed off on her; and how could she possibly explain that she had never thought, not for a moment, that they were being uprooted for good, even when they moved to the ghetto and had to leave everything behind, even then she hadn't quite grasped it. It appeared she was blaming him for something neither of them could define, perhaps for withdrawing from their company too soon and leaving her alone with the two of them. And maybe it wasn't anger she was feeling, but a form of distance that might exist only between two people who used to be very close. "I don't judge anyone who didn't think like me," he suddenly barged into her thoughts, as if resurrecting an old argument, and then fell silent. Hannah rose from her chair and began to collect the dishes. "I didn't think about them for the first few years," he continued. "I was entirely immersed in the present, in life on the kibbutz, in my work. Later, when I left, that changed." "Before the war began?" she asked. "Yes, before." "I have to put the little one to bed. It's already late," Hannah said. She helped Yoel gather the drawings from the floor and took him to his room. "I'll find an apartment as soon as I'm back on my feet," she told Jan once they were alone. "There's no rush, Elinka. Take your time." "Strange," she finally said. "What's strange?" "Sitting together after all these years." "Yes. I always dreamt about it, my little sister," he said again, and she could see how he looked at her with wonder, as if struggling to find the girl he knew in the serious, solemn woman sitting before him; and she asked herself whether he had truly dreamt about it, or whether he already regretted rushing to invite her into his home. "Everything will be okay," he said. "You'll see. People who came here after the war are building themselves a new life."

To turn the page, to start a new chapter, to make a fresh start, all those phrases were torn from the pages of a novel someone else had written. She studied him with a look reserved for people who addressed her in platitudes intended to move her, and he felt her turning to stone, realized she wasn't grasping what he was telling her, and that there was no point in continuing to encourage her, there was nothing she could do with it, not even weeks later, tucked safely inside a house with two parents and a child, reattached to the heart of a healthy, healing, forgiving humanity. "She doesn't have much patience for Yoel either," Hannah told him somewhat bitterly, observing that Elsa played with the baby reluctantly, out of a sense of duty and not joy; she felt sorry for her son, who insisted on fighting a battle his parents had already written off as futile. She felt embarrassed by the way Elsa's burning, cat-like eyes seemed to look not at them but through them, at hearing the moans that escaped her mouth late at night, mixing with Yoel's cries, but demanding to be left alone. The room remained shut and Jan adamantly forbade her from entering; "She mustn't know we can hear," he ruled. Hannah thought that perhaps they should send her to counseling. "She's not your enemy," he said. "Who said enemy? What does that have to do with anything?" "Sometimes I think you view her as an enemy." "I really think it would bring her some relief to talk to someone," she insisted. "How do we know that talking brings relief?" He knew Elsa would turn down the suggestion, there was no point in even asking her. Years later, when he decided to uproot his family to Australia, he told her: You don't know how similar we actually are, we're like a photo and its negative, your tight grip and my letting go stem from the same feeling of unrest, can't you see that? She didn't say a word, but for the first time she felt she understood what he was talking about.

She enrolled in Lewinsky Seminar and commenced her studies

toward a teaching certificate. During the same period she also worked to improve her Hebrew, until she gained a certain confidence and gradually eliminated the traces of her foreign accent. Going back to school wasn't easy. For a while she considered changing careers and switching to biology, but feared that for such a change it was too late, and she knew that teaching languages was her forte. The vast majority of the Lewinsky Seminar students were younger than her, Palestine natives who spoke Hebrew as a mother tongue and didn't know Europe, either its culture or its carnage. Most were about to get married, or were already married and with their first or second child, and had chosen teaching because it was a "convenient profession for women." She realized that teaching was the most normative profession here, and that her mere presence had an unnerving effect on them. She sought to spare them the awkwardness—by then she had already come to understand that what they called the Holocaust triggered great unease; she wanted neither their encouragement nor their silence. In the afternoons she tutored English and French, and three nights a week worked as a proofreader at the Hungarian newspaper *Új Kelet*. She began to save up money, which eventually allowed her to rent an apartment on A. D. Gordon Street, close to Jan and Hannah.

This was the contract she made with herself: a good, predictable routine, without veering right or left; a life without divergence, steady and unchanging, with no twists and turns. No kibbutz (several of Jan's old friends had tried talking her into moving to the kibbutz, where things would be simpler, more sheltered, but she didn't want to, she wanted a shut door and a stairway from which she could just nod hello and turn her back without apologizing; she had already gotten used to the functional, reserved, and unintimidating architecture of the white city of Tel Aviv, which posed neither dangers nor mysteries); no *Új Kelet* editorial board to burden her; no Voice of Israel radio programs in Hungarian. Then what did she want? Five days a week in the company of young people, under no circumstances children, youth at the threshold of life, whom she needed to somehow convince that she still had something valuable to give. That something had to be unconnected to her past. Thus, the idea of teaching English slowly took shape. English marked the limits of her ambition, a safe path, one that would enable her to support herself with dignity, provide for her necessities, and never make her feel dependent. Life was a collection of exercises she perfected, realms of activities and responsibilities that created the confined realm in which she was a teacher, *the* teacher, a title reserved for those who say what they do and do what they say. Failing to find her place in the post-war world, she delineated this very narrow space, in which she set the rules and everyone played according to said rules. She didn't want to be touched. She wanted to make her way among the masses, to carve a path like an industrial ant, which she would tread with her head held high, and without anyone brushing up against her, hugging her, or offering gestures of kindness. She had no need for such things. The words Hungary, Kolozsvár, Transylvania, would never again be uttered by her lips. "Do you want to visit?" Jan asked her several years after her arrival. "Are you insane? What for?" "What do you mean what for? To see the house. To see what's left." "I can't." Was it really possible to put it aside? Everything could be set aside. At first it seemed impossible. It seemed it would never relent. Later it became something cast in her image. It became her essence, in a way that allowed her to live in peace, serious, strong, professional, honest. That was the Weiss we came to know, years later.

There were moments when it seemed she was capable of more, wanted more, the glow of a sunset, a movie she had once seen, a book she had once read, a student she had truly loved, who was like a son to her (she never said that word, son, not even to herself); the memory of a postcard her parents had sent from a trip to Switzerland, waterfalls that resembled two families leading their children to a chuppah on the mountaintop, where the bride and groom would become one; but if she allowed herself to want, at that very moment it would become an excessive, gargantuan desire, a matter of life and death. There were years during which hope had flickered at the edge of her consciousness, making her believe someone might come if she didn't force it. But she did not fall in love even once. Here and there a spark, soon to be snuffed out. She moved across time like a person leaping at the task of cleaning his home, determined and purposeful, if not passionate. It wasn't passion that drove her. It was more like stubbornness. She was stubborn, and she insisted, among other things, on persevering. She denied herself all the good that people might bestow. Not because she found it to be false, but because she forgot it existed.

27

Had we read the story of another survivor from the Kastner train, we would most likely not have devoted a separate chapter to that public period in which the Kastner trial, and Kastner's subsequent murder, took place. Because for many of the train's passengers, those for whom the words "fresh start" or "new chapter" had meaning, those who gave everything they had to create a "new life" after the war, these events had passed them by without leaving an impression, and sometimes without even their full awareness. There were several people I turned to with the obvious question of "Where were you at the time of the trial?" who then opened their homes and hearts to me. "We didn't know Hebrew. We were busy surviving. We didn't always listen to the radio. No one had the time. I had three children. Not a trial or anything else could find its way in. And that applies to a lot of people my age from the groups that immigrated with me. We weren't aware of it. It was some faraway political business. We made it to Israel and tried to survive. Everyone had heard of the Eichmann trial. My daughter was in a stroller and I knew I couldn't tell the children I didn't want anything to do with it, you went outside and the radios were on everywhere and it's all you heard. I remember taking my girl and walking and walking and walking. I didn't want to hear it. Enough. No more."—This was recounted to me by a woman, a kibbutz member from Budapest who had boarded the train as a teenager, without her family. Another survivor, a religious man who lived in Jerusalem, also from Budapest, who was a boy when he boarded the train along with parents and several of his siblings, told me they, the train survivors, were no different from the other Holocaust survivors, that there was no reason to think they had reacted any differently. "You don't look back. We didn't busy ourselves with it. There were historians, legal scholars; the people who were in control here were the native Israelis. But there was serious business, to take care of life, to think of the future. There was no time and no means. I didn't think it was an essential part of my life. I didn't want to get into it. My children didn't know anything. That's how we were raised. You had to assimilate as quickly as possible and be like everyone else. I haven't summed up my life yet, haven't written an autobiography. It was news. I didn't ignore it, I read the papers, I listened to the radio. I wasn't capable of more. I haven't talked about this in decades."

But these events played out differently for Weiss. Upon her arrival in Israel, her life was split in two. For six years she managed to obtain a certain hard-earned peace. She began working as a substitute teacher in a high school uptown, before receiving a full time teaching position in our high school. Tel Aviv had become her home. She would finish work in the afternoon, come home, change clothes and dart down Ben Yehuda Street toward the boardwalk, equipped with a book she had borrowed from Mira, the librarian of Zamenhof, sit on a beach chair, or go to a matinee at the Eden or Esther cinema. Every so often, on the street or at a movie, she would bump into someone she had seen along her journey, on rare occasions even coming across people she knew from Kolozsvár, and nod, stop for a brief conversation, or gesture that she was in a hurry. They didn't appear eager to talk either. Every now and then she accepted Jan and Hannah's invitation to Friday night dinner, sometimes with other acquaintances. For the most part she preferred to stay at home.

She first heard of the trial on the Voice of Israel's Hungarian broadcast. She had read about Gruenwald's allegation and Kastner's libel suit in the newspapers, and thought it looked like a very sophisticated conspiracy, cynical abuse, just like in the Inquisition. When she raised the subject at Shabbat dinner, flushed with fury, Jan told her it was a tempest in a teapot, the controversies hadn't begun here but had broken out already in Europe; it had its own pace, the storm, ebbing and flowing, and none of it was worth one's health. She immediately rejected his position. That's exactly it, she replied, the people who orchestrated this setup have power and the only ones who can disprove it have none, because it has nothing to do with them, and the entire matter will stand or fall on that alone.

Not that it spurred her into action. It hit at the very heart of their helplessness, as Kastner had spared them any involvement from the beginning, unburdening them from the decision and the responsibility, as if it was possible to pull through it without being involved in one way or another. And she knew it was possible to remain uninvolved now, too, that is, to completely detach from it, categorically, as if it had never happened, or in any event, had never happened to her, because those were her options, either letting it possess you or fleeing from it, and she guessed, without having exchanged a word about it with any of her acquaintances, that most would choose detachment, she had enough presence of mind to see that no one had the time to deal with it, we're all sufficiently versed in complicity by now, she noted to herself cynically, not to lend a hand, not to bother, not to risk it; it's always been Kastner's own business, his own bravery, his own boldness, in which it was their privilege—or punishment—to be part of.

She read the headlines with disbelief, of Kastner "the failure who failed his people," who "sold his soul to the devil," of Kastner's defenders who "refute by mere words the hallowed truths and feats of bravery that served as a pillar of fire before the camp," and of the refusal "to draw a distinct line between the holy and the abominable." It could be said—she certainly thought it could be expected that one of them would say—that this man acted to save me, this man kept me from dirtying my hands, this man took all the dirt upon himself and got inextricably entangled with people he loathed. It could be expected and yet she didn't expect it; neither did she expect these questions to suddenly appear on anyone's lips. She admitted there were questions she had never asked herself—whether more could have been done for them from Palestine, whether they could have facilitated—whether they did anything to facilitate—their rescue. She found entirely perverse the idea that those who didn't act in fact aided the extermination, whereas the notion that everyone was corrupt was simply meaningless.

She found it odd, the courthouse, that stage, those voices; it was strange that someone else had broached the subject she herself had yet to find the strength to contemplate. It was strange that others thought they could say something about what she had experienced, and not because there was no good and evil in her world. There was. There was responsibility and irresponsibility, trust and distrust, generosity and greed. There was devotion. There was care. And she graded every move. She also didn't want to say people couldn't be judged on their past. Of course they could. She always believed reality itself was much more interesting than the judgment of reality, that people tended to judge reality because they feared it, as if seeking to hold onto it tightly so it wouldn't overwhelm them and their ideas about what ought to happen. It was clear to her that people who could afford to conduct this discussion and ask such questions were only those who were distant from the matter. Only from the outside was it possible to believe that chaos could be controlled, arbitrariness eliminated, order restored. In a sense, and she didn't dare say this to anyone, it was madness to bring this matter to court, a madness equivalent to the insanity that had brought on the original catastrophe. Obviously, she knew it wasn't really equivalent. That was precisely the type of sophistry she detested. But if the Revisionists could do it, so could she. So there. She was countering their vanity with her own, a vanity she only seldom revealed. A European, exilic, spiteful vanity, that suddenly made her wonder whom she hated more.

They used extreme expressions, heated, powerful words she had come to despise, words that clashed with life, with her life, which suddenly seemed so feeble and directionless in their presence. Never before had words been further removed from the phenomena they allegedly strove to reconstruct or describe or elucidate. Never before had such a distance been traveled, and with such arrogance, as if an evil eye had been spying on her wherever she turned, forcing her former life into a narrow prism. Now she no longer had a choice but to cross that abyss, to pass through those words if only to keep them at bay, to fight to keep everything she knew inside her from slipping away. But what really was it that she knew? After all, she never thought of it before, not like this. It wouldn't be true to say she didn't remember, but she didn't organize it in her head, and now it was forced upon her in some violent manner that confounded her wavering memory. Had she been on the witness stand she would probably have collapsed under the weight of her own contradictions. But she knew no one lied deliberately; certain people deluded themselves into thinking they knew more than others, like Eric and his friends in the beginning, or like Müllner and the people on the rescue committee, while the others, her parents and she herself and most of the passengers on the train, ascribed to them this exclusive knowledge just because they wanted it to be true and sought to maintain the hierarchy that, in normal times, divides society into those supposedly in the loop and those who know how to take care of their own. And yet there was no way of correcting what had been said at the trial and written in the papers because, in reality, and she understood this quite early on, it wasn't about them at all, the passengers; no one was really interested in them, not in their grief and not in their resentment; she could fight, hate, earn herself detractors, argue until she was blue in the face; but none of it would make any difference, and she chose to remain silent. She preferred not to rally or fight for Kastner's reputation—which she never doubted—nor for her own. She was nailed to her own life, trapped in her day-to-day, and wanted it to continue exactly the same way, letter for letter.

And it came at a price. It became a festering wound. She wanted nothing to do with them, with those institutions, she wanted never to hear from them again. Anything that had to do with the State, even years later, when they approached her to commemorate, to testify, when they called and pestered, invaded her home and took her by the throat, she wouldn't respond; anything that smelled like institutional agency, ceremonial consciousness, national pride, Yad Vashem, she utterly distrusted. The trial and the murder were the final dissolution. For the first time, she felt truly betrayed.

She was a victim, but not a pure victim, that's exactly it—if she had earned her life by negotiating with the Nazis, she would be an impure victim, an impure survivor, a tainted survivor. The pure victim was the guiltless victim, who was merely led; the honor of the led sheep was preserved, because his innocence was preserved, because he never came in contact with the slaughterers, apart from when being led to slaughter. The pure victim's fault was his sweeping passivity, his complete resignation to what was being forced upon him, his profound weakness. Blaming the tarnished victim was more complicated, since he was charged with a double passivity, both with regard to the slaughterers and to the leaders who had chosen, on his behalf, to be in contact with the slaughterers, in order to secure a deal. He facilitated that deal, which eventually saved his life. She didn't need Kastner's persecutors to awaken the demons' guilt, she was there, behind the barbed wire of Bergen-Belsen, a mere step between her and the horror, she didn't need anyone's help to feel contempt for her own helplessness. She hadn't wronged anyone, and yet carried the full weight of the sin. In a sense, she could only thank them, because they demonstrated the insanity embodied in the charge.

She didn't tell, most of them didn't tell and didn't testify. In the courtroom, only what could be named was relayed—wide movements across space and time, train stations, dates, people's names. But was it important? Where was the true reality? Did they leave any room for it? Who Kastner was was a question everyone supposedly tried to answer. But who were they? Could anyone answer her that? Did she herself have an answer? Who were those people, testifying while not testifying, who were those caught in the middle, thrust into the thick of it? "Those" who shared the same universe, lived, walked and talked inside it, as divided and idiosyncratic as they were; "those" who were either directly or indirectly scarred by collective guilt; "those" who picked up their suitcases and accepted the privilege of fleeing for their lives; "those" who knew-and-didn't-know that this privilege was a form of theft, a two-way theft in fact, depriving them too of the simplicity of being alive; "those" who eventually collapsed under the burden of an impersonal vendetta, lacking a palpable subject, which gradually also depleted them of that deep empathy that exists between people who live through a shared tragedy. Could anyone explain it, that mystery, which works precisely because it isn't fully aware of itself, because the manipulations and negotiations merely scratch the surface of the inner workings that remain hidden from view? But they wanted to let sleeping dogs lie, to leave it behind them, to move forward, to bury their heads in what the new routine had already begun to provide, if only to a few of them. Concealment was their second nature, not because they had anything to hide, but because no one was interested, there was no one to talk to, and those who did seemingly listen judged harshly for the sake of some inflated image they held of the pure victim, or better yet, the partisan, as a potential object of identification. The pedagogical notion that when you teach students about heroes you instill values of heroism, and when you teach them about the miserable souls who didn't know how to fight their fate you inevitably inspire feebleness, struck Weiss as entirely ridiculous. She didn't think there was any specific weight to the way people spoke, that it truly affected the choices of others, or that there was any educational value in superhuman or inhuman feats of bravery. She also didn't understand why only heroes counted, and she hadn't lived long enough in Israel to witness how the exilic mentality became, at least among certain intellectuals, a new form of resistance, a type of heroism—the mother of all sins. For her, the line didn't cross between the public and the leadership, between the knowledgeable and ignorant, the resisters and collaborators. She saw bravery and rebellion in hidden places. But of course, she didn't involve herself. She had no trouble justifying her avoidance. It was clear to her that she wasn't an educator, was never assigned a homeroom, as language teachers seldom were. They taught French or English and left the task of educating to the Torah, history, and literature teachers, and sometimes even to the math, physics, and chemistry teachers, God knows why. The language teachers were spared.

She didn't attend the trial. It never even crossed her mind. She was there in spirit. She stood trial vicariously, and was vicariously sentenced. And when he was shot and a few days later breathed his last, on the night of March 15th, 1957, she sobbed for hours. The murder of Israel Rudolf Kastner, whom she had never met in person, stirred up the demons of her orphanhood. She had never looked up to a leader, never pinned her hopes on anyone. He wasn't her hero. Weiss had no heroes. But she owed him her life, even if she wasn't sure of its worth. It was within her grasp and yet it eluded her.

Sometime back in the sixties she started teaching at our high school. Her Hebrew, which she had struggled with for the first few years, gradually improved and became refined. The number of people with whom she associated slowly diminished. She seldom received invitations, and rarely did any inviting herself. Every so often someone looked for her. Once in a while she was found. Here and there fate dealt her heart-rending encounters. Gradually, something inside of her steadied and calmed. But the nights were agonizing. She felt surrounded by suspicion and hatred, an unfamiliar hatred, harder to bear, the leadership's hatred, hatred toward the leadership, hatred toward the poor survivors, hatred that provoked her own hatred, conquered the terrains of love and at a certain point seeped into her teaching. Never directly. Weiss knew how to veil her inner turmoil.

Thus, she didn't start arguments, didn't defend herself, either in the late fifties or twenty years after, when we met her. She didn't initiate debates, not even fanciful, vulgar discussions revolving around questions such as what would have happened if; how would I have acted if; what led people to be hangmen or resisters; what would I have taken upon myself; what potential personality lurks inside me and in what way would it have manifested under circumstances I didn't experience and probably never will. She spared us these simulation games. But how does one defend one's character? By actions. The act she chose to perform was a complicated one. In each and every lesson, we were all collaborators. No one complained, no one protested. We allowed her to act as she deemed fit, even if she didn't stage these scenes deliberately. We accepted her whims as divine decree even when she punished the innocent. We tried to adjust ourselves each day anew. During all those years we studied under her we experienced firsthand the enigma of collaboration. It became the greatest enigma of our lives.

28

One morning she woke and went swimming in the pool as usual. Upon her return she saw a fire engine at the entrance of the building. Several neighbors were crowded downstairs and when they noticed her, ran toward her panting, "Ms. Weiss, Ms. Weiss, you left the gas on." A fire had broken out, they told her; Mr. Kahn from the second floor noticed the smoke coming from her apartment and knocked on Mrs. Lifschitz's door, who immediately called the fire department in order to salvage whatever was left to be salvaged, but the truck came too late, they informed her solemnly with worried expressions. Mr. and Mrs. Lifschitz climbed with her to the top floor. She thanked them and asked to be left alone. The front door was torn from its hinges. Inside it was blacker than black, her every possession dessimated due to a moment of carelessness. The apartment was insured, of course, as was all the furniture, everything except what made the apartment a home, her sanctuary. When she went out that morning she had even forgotten to take along her wallet, in which she kept the two photos of her parents.

Nothing remained. Not only the few photos that usually accompanied her, but hand-written letters from Mother and Father; the little farewell notes Mother had placed in her socks before her train journey, unbeknownst to her; letters from Jan she had kept from the time he left for Palestine and letters he sent her in Switzerland; the correspondence with Eric in Paris; birthday greetings she hurriedly retrieved from her jewelry box while packing her belongings and never even bothered to look at again, leaving them scattered in drawers, thinking one day she'd make time to read them; all the remnants of her past, all the signs that she had lived. The fire also consumed the rectangular picture she hung on the pantry wall, a gift Clara had made her when she was fourteen, which wandered with her from place to place, the cracked glass having been gently removed already back in Kolozsvár, leaving only the simple wooden frame to hold the yellowish, divided passe-partout; on the left side she had attached the figure of Chloris the nymph from Botticelli's Primavera, her lush golden hair flowing down her neck and shoulders, her eyes wide open, her gaping mouth blowing a sprig of flowers before Zephyrus, God of Wind, a moment before her transformation into Flora; on the right side she glued the portrait of The Lady with a Fan by Velázquez, a dark and doleful, pursed-lipped figure, her gaze pensive and sphinxlike.

Another holocaust divided her life and shattered its continuity, another holocaust she had experienced clandestinely, without telling almost anyone, another rupture that rendered her incapable of feeling anything but a daunting darkness, a profound sorrow, as if she had been stripped of her humanity and from now on must be grateful for every tear shed, every moment of overwhelming emotion. In the past, whenever she tried to conjure up the small holocaust—which is how she thought of it—of her youth, the sudden cessation of her passion that had disrupted her life before the big holocaust, she couldn't, even though she believed the small holocaust was the reason she couldn't get back on her feet after the big one. Others succeeded where she had failed. She wasn't moving forward, wasn't rising, the same way her energy suddenly drained from her at a young age, when it felt as though her options had all slipped through her fingers. You still have your entire life ahead of you, Jan told her upon her arrival in Palestine, you're young, he said as she studied him skeptically, as if he wasn't addressing her at all, as if he was talking about someone else.

But the fire forced upon her a more radical asceticism than she had already known. That very summer she was supposed to have visited Jan in Australia. She cancelled all her plans and took, for the first time, a week's leave in order to prepare for her move, fleeing to the prefabricated buildings in Bat Yam, near the neighborhood of Ramat Yosef—no one knew her new address. She now resided among the Jewish immigrants from Russia, Iraq, Poland, and Turkey cloistered behind grilled railings attached to monotonous concrete slabs, some of them Holocaust survivors her age and older. They immediately identified a kinship of fate—from which she also fled—and scowled at the stranger who refused to integrate into their community and turned down their invitations. Children were always horsing around at the entrance of the building when she returned home from an exhausting day at work. The staircase was filthy, exposed sewage pipes heightened the sense of neglect, and cats often managed to weave through the window bars and leave their tracks on her sheets. She barely furnished the apartment. The walls were whitewashed poorly and cracked from the humidity. She left the tiles bare of rugs, forwent hanging curtains and let the grills on the balcony mar her view. In the evenings she tried to map out her time, jotting down the names of television programs worth watching, since she was sometimes too distracted to read. She dragged out the process of grading papers, spending much more time on it than she actually needed. For an entire year she boarded bus number 26, which went from Bat Yam to Beit Eliyahu in Tel Aviv, an hour each way. She breathed a sigh of relief when the renovations of her apartment were finished and she could finally return home.

The more the landscapes of her memory faded, the more the longing gnawed at her heart. It was during those nights, after long days at the high school, sprawled on the agency bed she had purchased, that the girl returned to visit her—the same girl who stared with gaping and cheerful eyes at what was revealed before her for the first time, the girl who grew up in a time when there was no world, only the mighty walls of a home and a family among whom she strutted like a foot soldier, cutting paper stripes and pinning them to her sleeves, looking straight into the camera with a serious gaze that concealed a self-assured mischievousness. The girl who later appeared and came to her aid at camp, like her own loyal squire, ready to serve her the way she had once served Jan, attentive to every movement and sound. The one who slept peacefully beside the sliding door that separated her parents' bedroom from hers, a room prepared for her in honor of entering the first grade, painted entirely in lilac with patches of white on its tiny shelves; the desk, the backpack, the spotless shirt that was ironed in the afternoon and patiently waited to be put on the next morning. Her window faced the street. A bird had built a nest there. It was their shared secret, her and the bird's. She intuited that the nest mustn't be removed, that if she tossed it to the ground the bird would retaliate, it would rally an army of birds to declare an all-out war against the humans, and the humans would eventually be defeated because they didn't have beaks.

There was also a journal in which she tried jotting down memories, a few entries she had neither the strength nor courage to process, quickly stowed away in the desk drawer. On the first page she wrote two quotes by Simone Veil. "There is a point in affliction where we are no longer able to bear either that it should go on or that we should be delivered from it." "Every being cries out silently to be read differently." "Living among others is no longer possible," she wrote in one of her entries, and in another, "the greatest mystery of my life: living in the aftermath."

29

The hallucinations were out of character; she was rational after all, almost too sober. She didn't become ridiculous, had never been ridiculous, but her eyes had stopped seeing what was before them. The street filled up with old, familiar figures. They reminded her of people she had once known, but instead of greeting her with open arms, they waved their arms menacingly, they pointed at her behind her back, they plotted against her, plots that reminded her that she wasn't alone and would never be alone, even if she were to escape to the other end of the world they would never let her withdraw into herself, it was futile to try to stave them off, futile to convince herself she had forgotten them, futile to attempt to prove they had no meaning in her life and that the life they had granted her was equally meaningless—they would come to demand the gift they had bestowed upon her against her will. Her voice became hoarse, and once she closed her eyes, traces of thoughts immediately started chipping away at her sleep. It seemed as though someone was wandering around her house and soon they were many, swooping in like bats, plunging at the walls and closets, crawling on the floor and on the counter.

Who cares what he says, they tried to calm her agitated nerves after the run-in with the principal, Mr. Ben Ami, what does it matter what he said, let it go, Ms. Weiss, for your own sake, don't waste your energy on it. But he never apologized, and in fact, what he said was beyond forgiveness or atonement. Since her own silence did nothing to ease her mind, and it never occurred to her to address him directly, her distress only grew. One day she quietly signaled to a few teachers to follow her to the end of the hallway, and handed each one a note, only after they promised complete discretion. The notes had the number of a chief inspector in the Israeli police. She asked them to call him on her behalf, he had already been updated and knew what to do. They couldn't ask too many questions, fearing her reaction and the betrayal of her trust. She implied that she believed the law was on her side in this matter. She had been in Israel long enough to understand the power of criminal law here, and how she was being unjustly persecuted. She urged them to help find her persecutors and keep them away from her. For the first time, she spoke in terms of persecutors and persecuted. For the first time, she revealed to strangers something about the war raging inside her. For the first time, she realized how weak she was. She didn't want to be told to leave. No one would tell her to leave, but it's possible she envisioned banishment long before the potential banishers realized their own hidden or overt intentions, and had in effect already been banished, had already banished herself.

She lost her skin. Her compulsive, powerful determination still managed to conceal the helplessness. But she was scared to death. She waged a war over her soul and enlisted others in the battle, but they were too foreign, too distant, and were unable to appease her and show her there was a way out. She was inconsolable; they couldn't explain to her that what she needed, urgently, was a doctor and not a policeman. Once again they had to cooperate with her, to comply, to honor her wishes, to show her that they took her complaints seriously and were trying to pursue her persecutors. But they lost her anyway. They shrugged in the teachers' lounge, said she was crazy, had lost her mind. Blindness had joined blindness without anyone crying out or standing up for her, and she, for her part, did not train a single soul to navigate the labyrinth of her mind.

She went for a stroll in the yard. The abandoned bench in the rear garden was covered in beads of rain. She wiped it dry with her hand and sat down, rubbed her fingers against her warm breath, retrieved an egg sandwich from her briefcase that she had prepared that morning, removed the plastic bag and lingered for a long time. She wasn't hungry. The rain picked up. She had forgotten her umbrella in the classroom and considered going back for it, but didn't want to see their faces again. She hated them. She could say that openly now, at least to herself. They didn't irritate her, that would be too lighthearted; what she felt was a dark brew of rage and resentment. She didn't want to see any of them, didn't want to deposit any of her assets in their little hands. No one interested her, no one touched her heart. It wasn't entirely true, she knew that, but she wouldn't let doubt seep into her thoughts. The rain stabbed the bench like needles, soaking her thin coat and tousling her hair, and she knew she would never step foot in that place again. That word, never, pealed like church bells with the full force of the storm roiling inside her, which had once resembled passion and now revealed itself to be the dark end of a tunnel that offered the only way out. She wanted to die. She knew it as never before. She knew that was it, she had even known it the night before, when she woke up and stole a glance at the small mirror perched on the bookshelf in the living room, next to her makeup bag, before returning to bed. Now she sat with her head between her hands, pressing them against her ears in order to silence the deafening noise blaring inside, but nothing helped. For a long while she heard nothing but screams and canons. She gradually let go and then noticed that her entire body was convulsing, her teeth chattering, she couldn't stop the tears from rolling down her cheeks and smearing her heavy makeup, a desperate, unrelenting wail that cried out to keep away from her, to clear a path, to open the gate wide. For the first time, she noted to herself with certain satisfaction, she was escaping from school.

She crossed Ibn Gabirol Street and continued via Huberman to Gan Yaakov behind Habima Theater, stepping in the murky puddles that collected between the cracks of the worn sidewalk, passed by Tarsat and Ben Zion boulevards and turned onto her street. At home she realized she had forgotten to buy groceries. The apartment was a mess. She hadn't changed the sheets in weeks, hadn't washed the towels, hadn't rolled up her sleeves, taken a rag and bucket, mopped the floor and scrubbed the tiles as she used to regularly do, especially after the rare occasions when someone had visited. She took out trash bags from the under the sink and started throwing away everything within sight, the contents of the refrigerator, the pantry, student papers, the small wardrobe she had purchased after the fire, the few books that stood on the shelves, the chinaware, glasses, bowls; she moved from cabinet to cabinet, opening drawers and slamming them shut. The bags were heavy; there was no way she could carry them down to the dumpsters. She piled them next to the front door.

Night had fallen. She collapsed into the armchair. She heard fragments of a conversation. She told him she feared for Elsa, she was too naïve, how would she manage. She's simply so young, she doesn't understand the rules of the game yet. That's her problem, always was, she puts too much trust in people. Father said everyone is naïve these days, even the most cynical and practical among us. She didn't reply, her mother. And then she began to cry.

What brought her joy? Music, a childhood song, the face of a loved one, a view she must revisit before she leaves no matter what. She fumbled her way to the window, returned to the kitchen table, held onto it as if possessed, as if begging it to take her captive and refuse to release her; but with just as much dread, she let go. She was ready. She looked at the clock; it was past midnight. They barged in armed, yelling at the top of their lungs, she feared they would wake the neighbors, they chased her and threatened to shave her head again, to get back at her for abandoning them. She had no one to call, no one to talk to, Jan wouldn't understand, he never really did. She got up and walked, swaying from side to side. The walls were closing in on her; she paced the apartment from one end to the other as if balancing on scaffolds, as if having to bridge discrepancies in height, rubbing up against the walls, bouncing off them. Her legs faltered, she struggled to stretch them and slapped her thighs to cajole them into moving. She thought she heard the incessant ring of the phone. Then it stopped. An unimaginable weakness came over her. A cramp shot through her stomach all the way to her lower back. She was covered in a thin, translucent layer of sweat, felt it on her forehead, her back, her cheeks.

She had sought death many times throughout the years. Even in her youth. And in Switzerland. She had to be kept alive. She wouldn't let anyone tend to her, but something inside her didn't want to die, she knew that much as well. Not because she wanted to achieve something and needed more time. Not because she thought one day she would have a family of her own. What kept her alive? It was a mystery. It wasn't because her parents had sent her off with the command to live, that vague responsibility that tied her hands behind the curtain, it wasn't that contract, even though that was the story she had told herself at the time. She didn't know what protected her. But the pain was back, a violent pain devoid of all substance, unlike anything she had ever felt before toward something or someone, and she was unwilling to suffer any longer. I'm tired, Mother, she wanted to tell her, and heard her laughing at her, a chuckle tinged with disbelief. She tried closing her eyes to see her clearly, but it was futile, and then even her voice disappeared. She got to her feet, walked to the window, and opened it wide.

She had had such dreams as a child, of bursting forth, straight ahead, with all her might, crossing the living room and hopping over the dividing rail with great momentum, into the air, to hover between heaven and earth and, if only for a moment, conquer the laws of gravity. Those are dreams of flight, Jan had told her. She'd spread her wings and fly several feet above ground, soar over the streets she loved, circle Dizengoff and take a right on Ibn Gabirol, cross the road at a low altitude and continue straight to Shaul HaMelech Street, hovering close to the ground, but then fall, spiral down and be done with it. Simply done with it. She wasn't thinking of pain, wasn't afraid she would fail; she knew she would succeed, just as she knew other things in her life once she stopped allowing herself not to know. She looked outside, mesmerized by the lightning that flashed through the window. Her eyes shone.

For a moment, the lights went out. She thought about it briefly, then made her way to the fuse box outside the door, flipped the switch, and came back inside. She knew it was time to let go. The building's windows were insulated. No one heard the great scream that sliced through the air, no one saw the black body, a bird-woman who fell like a shooting star in the middle of the night.

30

Near the end of the 1981 school year, we gave her a gift, David Attenborough's book *Life on Earth*. She didn't expect our gratitude. She didn't expect that something of her hidden desires would be revealed to us. And suddenly it seemed to us that she was happy, happy to be acknowledged, like a distant relative attending a family ceremony of unwrapping presents and discovering she had not been forgotten, and the present was even to her liking. The gift we dared to give her baffles me even today. Did she understand at that moment that we loved her? And why would we give her a gift if not out of love? What was it if not a gift of love? She understood something, probably didn't hold onto it for long, but for a brief moment it was possible she let herself be loved. At the end of our last class, moments before everything was said and done, we wanted to stay with her in a place where it was possible to talk about love. This is for you, we brought you something. And she smiled.

She took the book, handling it as gently as a precious etrog before Sukkot, and unwrapped it bashfully and with wonder, visibly emotional. It was a tremendous vote of confidence, to accept a gift from us, to acknowledge the spontaneous gesture of our young hearts that held her in high regard, and not view it as a crude invasion of her privacy, an intolerable violation of the type of interaction she had toiled to uphold during the three years she taught us. She understood our need to give of ourselves to her, even though she had probably never expected us to cherish her hard work. We bought her something we were almost certain she would like. Obviously, we didn't know her home had emptied of books. We had no idea what kind of storm had been raging during those months and years in the teachers' lounge and in her life. We didn't know that she had been teaching us while the ground was shaking beneath her. She kept up appearances, as a teacher is expected to do. Summer rolled in. We enlisted in the army. On a weekend leave, about ten months into our service, a friend called me. "Did you hear what happened? Weiss killed herself."

Weiss took her own life. No one had anticipated the calamity, but once it transpired, it was perceived as the end of a chronicle foretold, or a divine decree, outside our scope of responsibility. The shock was reserved, dry, void of sentiment. Feelings of guilt or anger, which the defeated often store with those left behind, were suppressed and faded away. There were those who said, as if embracing her point of view, that a new generation of students had emerged—over the period of a single year—a strange and rude generation that didn't listen and didn't obey. "After us," they said, it was no longer the same, as if her life and death had truly been up to us. For some reason this explanation made sense to some of us, even though it didn't lead us to the obvious conclusion that in our absence, once we went our own way, we became her murderers. We hadn't mattered that much. The flip side of that same explanation was that it was an act of insanity, an act that the school promptly washed its hands of, and was the fate of a woman who had always made an exception of herself. The heavy silence that shrouded her life grew thicker surrounding her death. Life at school had resumed its course. A new teacher was found to replace her. It was the end of an era, an era she had presided over without ever assuming her position, without forging a vision, without setting the tone. She was the school.

31

During my years in Paris I taught Hebrew lessons each and every week at the Orthodox synagogue in the 19th arrondissement. I wore a long cotton dress, put on a wool sweater vest and arrived thirty minutes before class. By this time, the last of the employees and worshipers had already scattered. I received a key to the front gate and set up the classroom. The "Jewish Radio" would blare through the room day and night, even when the synagogue was closed. The desks were soiled with leftover scraps of food. I would wipe up the rivulets of drool that dribbled from the meaty lips of the synagogue beadle, who was prone to rest his head on the table for an afternoon nap without bothering to clean up after himself. In the corner of the room stood a cramped cubicle with hundreds of candies, canned foods, Kiddush wines, and a small fridge for the staff. Just before seven o'clock in the evening, around eight adult students would gather, most of them laborers and housewives, who lived in a type of voluntary ghetto in the arrondissement, some full of disgust and contempt toward Paris, others merely indifferent. Very few crossed the Seine to the Latin Quarter, visited the Louvre or d'Orsay or the Opéra Bastille. Only

Jerusalem inspired in them a passion for unequivocal justice and ignited a hatred toward its enemies, both real and imagined.

They knew nothing about me. My teaching was void of me; my experience and wisdom went completely unnoticed. Language transformed me into a conduit through which not a thing was shared with them, no thoughts, no passions, nothing of me. I welcomed them warmly, even though we shared nothing but the limited vocabulary and grammar that were completely tailored to their needs. They sought to learn everyday Hebrew so they would be able to get by in Israel, those who wished to immigrate, to understand the news on the radio, to shop and chat. I gave them basic exercises that demanded of me limited creativity, we learned songs and read articles out of *Sha'ar LaMatchil*, we walked along paved paths, the narrow margin of error easily lending itself to a slight correction or a lighthearted scolding.

We lived in an absolute present, with neither a past nor a future, speaking in a common language that didn't require us to bridge distances or take risks. We spent long hours together this way, without struggling, hours in which I knew contentment, though perhaps contentment isn't exactly the right word. Language made me happy, the verb conjugations, the pronouns, the practice, the innovation, the immediacy. I extended my arms enthusiastically whenever pointing to a particular verb, and asked them to conjugate it. Only when I left in the late evening did I contemplate how much effort I had exerted. Only then did a kind of heaviness color the pleasure. I felt I was going backward, as if I were becoming a child again and returning to a very early exchange of basic questions and answers in a native tongue, settling for useful signifiers and emptying my own language of meaning and ideas. Here and there I betrayed the traces of more ancient studies, when

I raised my hand in an overdramatic gesture that didn't suit the dimensions of the words uttered, but rather the dimensions of a different saying, one that was no longer in my lexicon.

In those years, I didn't think of Weiss, or of the fact that I was treading the same paths she had once tread. It seemed she had disappeared from my consciousness and cleared the way for other teachers. I never asked myself questions about her, a fact that undoubtedly had to do with the way she appeared, with her uncompromising demand on the living present, with the warning she sent our way, both directly and indirectly, to refrain from knowing her. The teacher would find a way to tell us everything we needed to know about her. To try and sidestep her, to expose her secrets, would have meant betraying her. And anyway, if she did have mood swings, they went unnoticed. It is possible that we didn't attribute to her an inner life. She protected us from her by making sure to teach us "only" the required material and not create any situation that might lead her to say things she would later regret. It was impossible to identify with her or wish to resemble her. She didn't serve as a role model, and I believe I wouldn't be mistaken if I said that none of her students followed in her footsteps. She was someone you didn't want to resemble, a manifestation of pure element, almost inhuman, in a certain sense asexual, preceding any sexual distinction, to which our reaction was primeval and subject to volatile shifts between attraction and repulsion. She dictated a different principle, which I tried to trace back decades later, a different lesson I tried to understand, had to understand, wanted to learn, but with a different kind of knowledge, one that was neither historical nor objective. I allowed for the possibility that at the end of that process I might come to know more about myself than about her. I wondered whether I too would desperately want to throw myself off the roof.

We met her when we were young enough to still be able to dismiss her as part of the intrigue called high school. We told ourselves that life, our lives, would start after, even though we kept postponing that starting point. When did we in fact begin to live? When we began studying with her she already had thirty years of teaching English under her belt, five or six days a week, and yet nothing about her showed any wear. She was fresh, sharp as a tack, and fulfilled her duties as faithfully as ever. The connection with the students was important to her, the one thing she didn't renounce. Did she derive pleasure from the generations of students, from the rows of ever new faces? Don't give up on it, I was also told more than once, leave yourself at least one class for the sake of Eros. Draw strength from them, for they give strength. And it was true. With time I could appreciate this power, the force that remains stored inside you even after you step out of the classroom, and that slowly dissipates the further you withdraw, submitting to other forces.

Did teaching fan the flames of life for Weiss too? Did it validate her? Was that why she persevered in it? Did I ever detect in her gaze the simple joy over the fact that we existed, we, always we, always in plural? If we were supposed to cure her, we failed, or she failed to imagine what might have cured her. Did she not understand what was happening to her? She was endowed with such vast curiosity, but she never even tried to understand herself. She made sure only to go through the motions of speaking, quite literally.

32

Time healed no wounds, though one might have expected it to, as part of the natural healing process. Time did not mend the wounds; they reopened. It's possible that was, in Jean Améry's withering words, Weiss's personal protest against the "natural," "immoral" healing that time brings about. She was forced to look back, to dive into the abyss again and again, to look her sudden, violent, inevitable end in the eye, to take leave without saying goodbye as if she were a cloud of road dust, as if she was entirely meaningless. And how could she possibly live longer than her parents had, she who spent her entire life as nothing if not their daughter.

I said at the beginning that she had died. There was no point in hiding it, in deceiving the readers. I had the starting point. Elsa Weiss was dead. I had to invent her a life. But how do you invent a life? I searched for her in vain. I didn't find her. I looked for her out in the world, but she didn't appear in any of the history books of the period, either by her first name or her last. Nor did she appear in any of the few memoirs and journals published about life in Bergen-Belsen, as if she had faded from memory, and been rendered invisible. I tried to locate distant traces of her young face in the few photographs that remain from the beginning of the journey, from the platform in Budapest, and upon the train's arrival in Switzerland. There is no sign of her. She was never in front, never stuck her head out the window, as if she had already curled up inside one of the cars and asked to be left alone, as if already then she had destined herself to be present only in the classroom. As if already then she had lent herself to the blessed fading of memory. This history must be searched for elsewhere, not in books. It is only when you listen to the oral tradition, a tradition that does not impart anything directly, does not convey content or teach in the traditional sense, but rather points out a place on the world map, a place that once upon a time had left its impression in a hidden corner of her students' consciousness; the place of the teacher. You can wander to this place. You can also never meet it again. You can spend an entire lifetime and forget you ever visited it. It is possible to take into account, in all my journeys from here on, that I had once stumbled upon that place, which suddenly demands to be put in writing.

I felt uncomfortable suddenly being so close to her, almost breathing down her neck. She, for her part, eluded me, wouldn't give in to me, only instructed me with her hands, with her eyes, to stay away, to make do with only what was necessary. But what is necessary in a person's life? I don't know. The allegedly peaceful routine, or perhaps the crises that brutally interrupt it? The liberties I took frightened me. I gave her a different name. I drew certain people close to her, and kept others away. I mostly kept them away. I thought she wouldn't tolerate too many people around her.

The world turned back on its axis again. I could roam freely from place to place. From an escape route, Europe had become a destination for me, a place that would perhaps offer shelter. I visited the building where she had lived in Tel Aviv. But was there anything in that building, in the apartment closed off to visitors, in the sun-scorched balcony railing, in the rickety shutters, that could shed light on the enigma that was her life? Could her house in Kolozsvár, in which she was born about a century ago, solve the riddle? Or perhaps it could be solved only by the sea and the pool, her two brave allies?

I could only fumble around her, to become acquainted with people who had most likely lived in her vicinity, a few bunks, boxcars, or hotel rooms away. I went to talk to a few of them. Wherever I went the door opened wide, I was greeted warmly, refreshments were served; never before had I felt in this country such—what I was embarrassed to call—solidarity, simple camaraderie. They remembered more than anything how they tried with all their might to stave off the memories, how busy they were surviving, how they tried to learn the language, to acclimate, to assimilate, face forward, to the future. And no, none of them had even noticed her. Odd. But she was so beautiful in her youth, I protested. Didn't she stand out? Was there no one who even resembled her? How did they not turn their heads when she walked by? I visited the high school. Tel Aviv is a frenetic city, always charging ahead, embracing one day and alienating the next. The security guard looked at me suspiciously. I used to be a student here, I said, I graduated shortly before the First Lebanon War. Why do you want to come in? he inquired, and asked for my ID card while informing the secretary, who, in turn, approached the principal to approve the visit. Finally I was let in. The old building remained standing, although a new one had been added in the interim. The old building is a three-story

U-shaped structure; the hallways have been whitewashed several times since the early eighties, the old combination of light green and faded yellow has been replaced with a more subtle color blend of eggshell and white. In many areas the floors remain the same, Terrazzo tiles polished by the soles of thousands of shoes. In each classroom I counted twenty-two student desks, forty chairs, a modern whiteboard where the old green chalkboard used to be, and hanging right beside it, in every classroom, a reproduction of Israel's Declaration of Independence. The windows are trapped behind the same bars, which have been repainted in pink, yellow and red. The backyard, the more intimate one, still more or less resembles itself with the olive tree, the fallen fruit of the ficus, the patches of dry grass, a few more benches scattered about. We sometimes studied Torah and Jewish history classes here, under the open sky. "In blood and fire Judea fell—in blood and fire Judea shall rise." The front yard is a wide concrete slab. I wandered between the floors, unable to find any mention of her; in fact, there is no trace of anyone who used to teach here, no commemorative book or plaque. I stood behind the front door of a classroom for a few minutes and tried to recall her voice. I decided to climb to the roof. It often seemed to me that of all animal locomotion, flight is the only movement possible for humans. I felt like I could fly, albeit not at a great height. I could only bear the low altitudes. Skyscrapers terrified me, I wouldn't even dare look out the window. I had to steady myself by gripping the railing, as if beyond it lurked something between a threat and a temptation.

I knew that the Kastner affair lay at the heart of the matter, but also that it was on the margins, like a distraction, that Weiss had happened to have found herself on that train just as she had happened to go along with everything else that came her way, and could just as easily not have boarded it. I learned of the story of the train by chance, one Holocaust Memorial Day, when I found myself at a memorial service for the survivors of the Kastner train, on Emanuel Haromi Boulevard, not far from my house, where Kastner had lived with his wife and daughter, and where he was murdered. When I got home, I knew. I knew with a complete confidence that I cannot explain. I went onto the Kastner website, searched for the passenger list, which numbered one thousand eight hundred and sixty-four. And there she was, among them, the teacher. I had to probe further. I drove to Jerusalem, to the Israeli television archives in Romema, and asked for a documentary about Kastner, which had been aired about two months after Weiss's death. With a pair of headphones I sat in front of a tiny screen and turned up the volume. One of the speakers was a young woman, the daughter of this murdered man, and suddenly I felt as though I was hearing my own voice, a voice determined to speak uninterrupted, while trying to suppress a slight, almost inaudible tremor. I heard a voice asking to survive in a world not trying to silence it, but actually instructing it to speak out loud. I heard a voice fighting to preserve its whispers, its hesitations, as though I had tricked myself and came from behind, from the past, from the mouth of another woman. It was my own voice coming through the headphones, even though I couldn't remember what I said, or who said what while she spoke in my voice. Only that it was my father whose reputation I was fighting for, and suddenly I was the daughter of the murdered man. I was dumbfounded. I didn't rewind the film to see to it again. But even my own words I can't always recall.

And the teacher's words, too, were as if they had never been.

33

In the second dream she stood at the blackboard jotting down things that pertained to texts Freud had written in the twenties. The blackboard was soft, malleable, as if made of Playdough, a receptacle-blackboard, a womb-blackboard, which she did not only write on, but became one with as it set no boundaries. She could sculpt it, pour into it, even bake in it. She stuck her head in and out of it as if playing, and the blackboard swallowed her whole; she merged with the words and the material, a single mass, a body from which she emerged and into which she faded, a magic notebook that cast her words in her image and absorbed the residues with a unique work of conceptualization that allowed her to witness how her own concepts were created, singular, hers and hers alone. She burst into wild, unexpected laughter, clearly elated and relishing the quiet harmony she created with her tool. And yet, the words were contorted and creased, ingested and spit out, losing their shape to render her text illegible. I was supposed to copy them down and asked myself what I would do if she quizzed me; maybe I'd borrow someone's notes before.

The class took place in my father's old study, in an apartment on the ground floor of a residential building on Bloch Street that had been converted into an office. To the right of the entrance was a spacious room with bookshelves mounted on a blue wall. Weiss presided over the lesson against volumes of verdicts and law and administrative ordinances, which served as the blackboard. We sat or stood opposite her, next to the desk, leather chair, and wide window, in an area opening into a yard leading to the dumpsters—I don't know who we were, or how many of us there were. Outside the office, along the corridor leading to the waiting room, were a cramped, unrenovated bathroom and kitchenette. It was the back room, the area outside the law, narrow and dark, damp and moldy in the summer, cold and oppressive in the winter, smelling as if it had absorbed decades' worth of urine, mildew, and bleach. A grilled window faced the backyard and the heart-wrenching scuffles between the courtyard cats. Weiss furiously erased the blackboard. She left us in the room and went to the bathroom, from which sounds of intestinal distress emerged. We remained frozen in place. She returned seething, "What filth."

She seemed so real. I saw her up close. She returned just as she had left, standing an arm's length from me, as if in resignation, as if giving in, turning herself in, giving into me, revealing herself without inhibitions so I would finally understand something I refused to understand, or was incapable of understanding. And then a discouraging sorrow spread over me at the thought that I was stalking her, pursuing her, chasing the one who wouldn't be caught, who evades any representation. I knew she wanted to tell me something, that I had to understand something beyond her. How far can I go, how far do I have the courage to go, where do I stop, whether knowingly or unknowingly? Weiss taunted me, and perhaps sought to dissuade me, to stop the search. Enough, let go. From this point on you must not know. And also: from this point on, don't even try to invent.

34

I was uncertain. It could still be a mistake, I told myself, until I reached her grave in the cemetery in Holon. The timeworn headstone had turned gray, coarse, and filthy. The black letters, etched in Hebrew and English, had gradually eroded as if adhering to a gnawing mechanism of self-erasure, destined to one day fade into the stone entirely, like a memorial for an anonymous soldier whose place of burial remains unknown, a monument that is a straight vertical, a right angle, pure shape. I had to move closer to read the names of her parents, Shmuel and Leah Bloom. Their daughter, Weiss by marriage, appearing by her full name, just so, on the list of train passengers, literally took her leave from the balcony into the air and downward, to the earth, thirty-eight years after the night they parted from each other in Kolozsvár, on Sunday, March 28th, 1982, a few hundred meters from Rabin Square, still Malchei Yisrael Square at the time. By then she was only Weiss, a lonely woman without a first name.

There are no possessive determiners on the headstone inscription: not our mother, not my sister; neither our teacher nor my teacher. Students are not in the habit of purchasing burial plots for their teachers. The material aspects of burials are the family's intimate affair. Whereas it is incumbent on the students, qua students, to appoint themselves a teacher and put in a plea for their salvation in her absence, to talk to the dead teacher. As Paul too ordered his Christian students in his Epistle to the Philippians: "Therefore, my dear friends, as you have always obeyed—not only in my presence, but now much more in my absence—continue to work out your salvation with fear and trembling." Thus, he had captured both wings of the disciples: with one wing they attempt to glide by appointing them a teacher in their image and in their likeness. They once again reflect upon the teacher's soul, which enfolds all of his teachings—how little they remember of the materials taught—in order to grow, to become different from who they are. With the other wing they break their flight, trembling and pleading before him.

Weiss didn't open any doors in her lifetime. Even the door to her grave she locked. Don't call on me, the worn inscription warns, fending off her visitors. Farewell, don't come searching for me, her last testament and nonexistent will says, demanding the impossible: to be anonymous within her name, to be a no-woman inside the name that precedes her. What do they command us, those who leave without a will, those who interrupt their lives and disappear from ours in a single night? What ultimate lesson would they have wanted to impart?

The grave told me, Leave. The grave drove me away. Without uttering a word, it told me about a woman who does not wish to be remembered, a woman who wishes not to be, and never to have been. The grave said, Find a different way. There ought to be a different way. I stood for a long while. I leaned in to listen. "Every being cries out silently to be read differently." That's what I think I heard.

Notes

Page 34: Who's got such a little girl, / such a little angel? / Eyes like two stars, / A pure little soul. (Yiddish lyrics by Janet Fleishman, music by Herman Yablokoff)

Page 38: "Dear God, I beg of you."

Page 39: Neolog Judaism was the name attributed to the non-Orthodox branch of Hungarian Jewry.

Page 54: James Joyce, "Eveline," featured in Dubliners, published 1914 by Grant Richards Ltd., London.

Page 67: Love of country is our law.

Page 69: To work is to pray.

Page 74: Assholes.

Page 79: A nickname given by the women and children to the female S.S. officers, from "Bergen-Belsen Diary" by Szondi.

Page 159: Simone Weil, *Gravity and Grace*, Translated by Emma Crawford and Mario von der Ruhr, first published in Routledge Classics 2002.

Acknowledgements

To my teachers and friends: Yosef Brucker, Tzipora Rimon, Nahum Sagi, Arieh Barnea, Daisy Hefner, David Frenkel, Ofra and Yitzhak Katzir, Gilly Sinita.

To Sari Kivistö and the Helsinki Collegium for Advanced Studies.

To my friends Naama Tzal, Dana Olmert and Shira Hadad, for their lucid and enlightening readings of my manuscript and all their help.

To Oded Wolkstein, my editor, a master magician and kind soul.

To my Dana.

Michal Ben-Naftali was born in Tel Aviv in 1963. A writer, translator, and editor, she has published collections of essays, a novella, a memoir, and a novel, as well as many articles on literature, philosophy, and art, in Israel and abroad. Her translations from French to Hebrew include works by Jacques Derrida, André Breton, Marina Tsvetaeva, Maurice Blanchot, Julia Kristeva, Esther Orner, and Annie Ernaux. She has received the 2007 Prime Minister's Prize, the 2008 Haaretz prize for Best Literary Essay of the Year, and the 2016 Sapir Prize for *The Teacher*. Her latest book, *A Dress of Fire*, was published in 2019.

DANIELLA ZAMIR lives in Tel-Aviv, where she works as a literary translator. She obtained her bachelor's degree in literature from Tel Aviv University, and her master's degree in creative writing from City University in London.

**OPEN
LETTER**

WWW.OPENLETTERBOOKS.ORG

**OPEN
LETTER**